A Famiglia Novel

DARK DESIRE

A.J. DANIELS

Dark Desire is a work of fiction. Names, characters, businesses, places, events, and incidents are either the product of the author's imagination or used in a fictitious manner. Any resemblance to actual persons, living or dead, or actual events is purely coincidental.

Cover Design and formatting by: ©Just Write. Creations

Edited by: Ansley Blackstock

ISBN: 978-0-9958409-4-2

BLURB

Klara

Everyone always says love will find you when you're not looking. Well, they're not wrong. Except, the man my heart stupidly fell for was more interested in playing his own twisted game of catch and release. Claiming me for himself, then pushing me away when I got too close, but there was an aura of darkness clouded around him.

A darkness that beckoned to me.

A darkness I was grateful for when those he thought he could trust ripped me away in the middle of the night to be a pawn in their own sick, twisted game.

Braxton

She was supposed to be an itch I needed to scratch. That red dress and those pale blue eyes called to me like a siren. In my line of work falling in love is dangerous.

"I believe there's good in you, Brax," she had said.

"Baby, I'm the thing monsters are afraid of," I warned her.

I pushed her away, thinking she would be safe from this fucked up life I lead.

I couldn't've been more wrong.

My enemies smelled fresh blood. They knew if they wanted to take me down, they had to get to her. But it wasn't my enemies I had to worry about. No, the threat was a lot closer than I thought. It shouldn't have surprised me. After all, the devil was once an angel. Klara was my light out of this hell, and now she was in danger of being snuffed out. But not if I could help it. They should've thought twice before taking what belongs to me. Now, I'm out for blood, and I'm not stopping until my concrete floor runs red.

ACKNOWLEDGEMENTS

Thank you to J.M. Walker, Dee Garcia, Ansley Blackstock, and V. Theia for letting me run scenes by them and taking the time to give me their feedback. You ladies rock! And I'm extremely grateful that I met you ladies and can call you friends.

Thank you to Teolia, and Laurie, my betas and ARC team who took a chance when I told them that this was different from anything I've written before.

Thank you to you, the reader. You didn't have to pick up Dark Desire, but I'm extremely grateful that you did.

Trigger warning: scenes of sexual assault.

"I'd cut my soul into a million different pieces just to form a constellation to light your way home.

I'd write love poems to the parts of yourself you can't stand.
I'd stand in the shadows of your heart and tell you I'm not afraid of your dark."
– Andrea Gibson

PROLOGUE

THE RIPENED SMELL body odor and human waste are the first things I notice as my body stirs. The old, stained mattress I'm lying on is the next. Followed by the sounds of harsh grunts, skin slapping against skin, and anguished cries.

I groan and try to find a position that alleviates at least some of the tension in my body, but it's no use. Everything aches. My arms from being tied above my head for god knows how long now. My legs from being violently pushed open day in and day out since I was dragged into this hell. My wrists from constantly pulling against the metal that's holding me captive. My heart with the cold realization that this is my life now. Nobody has come for me in the three months since I was taken.

The curtain separating my small section of the room screeches open, and I brace myself for what comes next. Before today I would've fought. Fought with everything I have left while cold fingers ripped the clothes from my body. While man after man did whatever they pleased with me. Sometimes one at a time, sometimes more.

But never, not once, did they ask for my consent. Not like I would've given it to them anyway. I was taken from my bed in the middle of the night. Sold from person to person until I ended up in this dark hell.

The smell of cigarette smoke and stale beer drifts down from above me as hands rip the blanket away from my body—the only thing I was allowed to cover myself with. I refuse to open my eyes because if I did... if I allowed myself to take in this new reality I would surely pray for death.

But with my eyes squeezed tightly closed I can drift away to another time. A time filled with love and laughter. When the only thing warring in my head were what classes I wanted to take.

The curtain screeches open again and I squeeze my eyes closed harder, but then the heavy weight above me becomes less and less, until there's nothing.

Slowly, wearily, I open one eye, and then the other. A silhouette of a giant stands at the entrance until he comes closer. One step, two steps. Then he's standing above me, chest heaving, nostrils flaring, fists clenching, but for reasons unknown to me, I don't flinch away. No, instead I stare down the giant. Emerald eyes into grey ones.

He grunts, bending down and pulling a tool from his pocket. I try shifting away, well, as far as my restraints will allow but he places a gentle hand on my arm. I frown looking at his monster sized hands, not understanding how they could be so big, so strong, and yet touch me with such gentleness.

"Going to cut you out of these," the giant says in a deep voice.

I nod, anxious to get the feeling back into my arms, to be able to move them in front of me, to be able to shield myself from further threats. But when he cuts through the binds, my arms don't move. Panic starts setting in, my eyes round in fear, and I can't get air in my lungs fast enough.

"Shit," he curses, gently pulling my arms down and in front of me, but I still can't feel them. Why can't I feel them? "Going to take a while until you get feeling back in them, baby girl. Hold on, going to get you out of here now, yeah?"

I swallow hard as his arms slip under me and lift me, bringing me into his hard chest. I can't help it. I burrow into him as close as I can get and take comfort in his warmth.

My   first   taste   of   comfort   in   months.

PART 1

ONE

Klara

"GET READY, BIACH! 'Cause we're going out tonight!" my best friend and roommate hollers, the front door slamming shut behind her causing the picture frames to rattle against the wall.

I groan and try to become one with the couch and the blanket covering me. "Dri, I don't think I want to go out tonight. My head is pounding, and I really don't feel good."

"That's why I got you these." She digs through the grocery bag hanging from her wrist before rearing back and pitching a box at me. I quirk an eyebrow at the cold meds and look up to see a smug grin on her face. "Take a couple of those and you'll be good to go."

"I don't know, Dri. Cold meds and alcohol shouldn't be mixed."

I know I should stick to my insistence on not going but the more Adrienne tries to convince me to go, the more my resolve melts away. I mean, it's just one night, right? I'll take the cold meds now, and by the time we hit the club I should be okay enough to have one drink. One drink, that's it. I owe my best friend this anyway after blowing her off last weekend so I could finish a paper early.

"Alright. Okay, I'll go." I pull back the blanket and grab the box of cold meds from the coffee table before making my way to the bathroom and the hot shower that awaits me.

Adrienne and I slide into the waiting cab an hour later. It only took about two point five seconds, and a side-eye perusal from the cab driver for me to realize that the crimson red dress Dri had picked out for me was way too short, barely covering my private parts when I sat down.

As soon as the driver pulls away from the curb, I try—unsuccessfully—to pull at the hem of my dress in hopes that I can wrench it down an extra inch or two. But all I'm doing is pulling the top down even more. The top that's barely covering my above average cleavage.

Ugh, tell me again why I agreed to go out tonight, and not just that, but why I let Dri dress me?

The only explanation I have is that the cold meds were starting to kick in, and I was not fully in control of my decisions.

"We're here."

Dri is radiating pure excitement as the cab pulls up to a…warehouse?

"Um, Dri? I don't think this is right."

"Just trust me, Klara," she says, paying the driver and grabbing my hand to pull me out behind her.

She yanks me out of the cab so fast that I have to scramble to try and keep my dress pulled down past my ass, but it's useless, and I'm pretty sure I just flashed the driver. Not like he was complaining though.

Fuck a duck! Just kill me now, please.

Dri's long, chocolate locks swish from side to side as she pulls me along behind her and up to a— oh, dear god the man is huge—bouncer. At least I think he's a bouncer. A sliver of fear races down my spine. I'm not liking the feel of this so far. This doesn't look anything like a club. Where's the lineup of people? Where's the velvet rope? Why are there absolutely no people outside, except for the huge mofo standing in front of us under the lone street lamp.

Dri and the dude don't exchange any words as she shows him a business card, and he nods, stepping back to pull open the heavy steel door with a squeak.

"Um, Dri —" I grip her hand tighter in mine and halt her advancement.

"It gets better inside, I swear," she promises, drawing an invisible cross over her heart. The gesture makes me giggle. It's the same gesture we've been doing ever since we were kids. When we made promises to each other we would say, "cross my heart," and draw the invisible cross over our hearts. It meant more to us than a pinky promise. We may have grown up, but that gesture still meant as much to us now as it did back then.

"Ugh, fine." I give in and let her lead me further into the darkness. "But remember, I don't have to be a fast runner, I just have to out run you, and judging by those shoes I'd have no problem." I grin.

Dri laughs, but her response gets cut off when the dark hallway finally opens, revealing a nightclub the likes of which I've never seen before – which isn't saying much, but still it's impressive.

My jaw drops taking in the crystal chandeliers hanging from the high ceilings. If it weren't for the DJ's lights, the illuminated bar, and the black light focused on the dance floor the entire place would be encased in darkness. The black walls run seamlessly down into black stone floors. Dark, blood red velvet curtains separate what I'm assuming are the VIP booths from view of the rest of the club.

"Holy –" I can't finish my sentence. I'm still trying to take everything in and process what I'm seeing. I was not expecting this when we pulled up to the seedy building.

"Right?" Dri asks, a wide grin splitting her face. "C'mon, let's get a drink, and then I'm dying to hit that dance floor."

She practically bounces down the stairs, through the throng of dancing bodies on the dance floor and over to the bar, dragging me—albeit willingly now—behind her. Dri pushes her way through the three people deep line at the bar and leans over more than is actually necessary, immediately catching the attention of the bartender, and eliciting scowls from the other patrons waiting to place their drink orders.

Shivers rain down my spine when I feel eyes on me. I crane my neck from side to side trying to get a lock on the culprit but when I don't see anyone blatantly looking, I shrug it off and accept the drink Dri is pushing into my hands.

"Right, it's dancing time," she announces, pushing past me on her mission to the middle of the dance floor.

Why do I feel like I'll be the one following her around all night? Oh right, because I'm pathetic, and although going out dancing once in a while with Adrienne is fun, this just isn't my scene. I so obviously don't belong here. I'd rather be back at home, curled up under my gravity blanket with a good book and a big steaming mug of coffee.

But live and let live, right?

Plus, Adrienne and I haven't been able to spend as much time as we'd like with each other over the last year. What, with both of us writing a thesis this year for our respective degrees, and work on top of that. We've been ships passing in the night lately. Sharing an apartment, but never really seeing each other except for the occasional, 'Hi. Bye' scenario.

I miss my best friend something fierce, so if this is what she wants to do, then I'm happy that I get to be here with her tonight.

I find Dri on the dance floor just as the DJ starts spinning the CID version of TLCs Creep. She giggles when I move closer to her and start grinding against her. We look like a couple dancing a little too close but neither one of us cares. Dri spins around into me, draping an arm over my shoulder as the song switches to Jax Jones's Instruction. I can't stifle the laugh when Dri dips down low and seductively dances her way up against my body.

I haven't felt this carefree or laughed this hard since before my parents' car accident that took them from me. It feels good and I hope I can hold on to the feeling a little longer. Two songs turn into four and before we know it both of us are sweating, our feet aching in our heels.

"Going to get a drink. You want one?" Dri yells above the music so that I can hear her. I nod and point my thumb over my shoulder to an open booth in the corner in a silent communication for her to meet me over there with the drinks. She grins and gives me a thumbs up before moving towards the bar.

Just as I'm about to turn around, I still. I feel his eyes on me long before the unmistakable scent of wood and spice and pure man invade my senses, and I sense him behind me.

"About to cause a fight in this club with the way that dress is riding up, Mia Bella." A low growl sounds near my ear, making my core clench. His warm breath causing goosebumps to appear on my skin.

"Hmm, not my fault if they don't know how to control themselves," I bite back.

He chuckles, a warm solid, very manly hand curling around my hip, while the other brushes my long ash-blonde hair from my shoulder.

"It's not them you have to worry about, babe."

His voice. Dear Lord, that voice. It's like silk, and sex, and that first bite of Lindor chocolate as it melts against your tongue. I gulp and turn around, making sure to not back away too far for fear that he might remove his hand from my hip and I'd lose the heat searing my skin at the contact.

"I'm not your babe, babe."

My eyes—the traitorous bastards—take in the dark leather shoes, dark dress pants, black button up shirt with the top button undone, sleeves rolled up revealing tanned, toned forearms, lips tipped up in a smirk. And oh, sweet Jesus, what I wouldn't give to tug on that full bottom lip. A little more than a five o'clock shadow, and then finally dark, amused eyes.

He chuckles, and it's deep, raw. "Drink."

"Huh?" I tip my head to the aside. I was so busy sizing him up that I didn't catch a word of what he said.

"Another drink?"

I can't help but stare when his tongue licks along his bottom lip, and suddenly images of him running that tongue down my neck, around my nipples, and over my clit flash in my mind's eye. My thighs clench.

TWO

"**O**NLY GOING TO ask you one more time, Mia Bella. I don't like to repeat myself." His voice was a breathy whisper against my heated skin as he ran his nose up the curve of my neck, inhaling my scent. "Can I interest you in another drink?"

I gulp and try not to think about how close he is, and the heat radiating from his body, and what it would feel like to be pinned beneath said body. "Um, I'm okay. One was my limit tonight."

He grins but doesn't try to push the matter which earns him a point in my book. I hate when guys insist on buying me another drink after I've said no.

"Keep me company while I get a refill then?"

My heart races and my belly does a little flop. What the fuck was that? Is it normal to have this kind of reaction to a perfect stranger? I don't even know his name, and despite my lack of experience, if he asked me to leave with him tonight, I know without a doubt that I probably would. Not because I'm eager to discover what exactly lies beneath the expensive suit—well, maybe it's a bit of that too, okay, it's a lot of that too—but because of how he's making me feel.

I've been in close proximity to him for less than five minutes and he's already managed to elicit more certain feelings in me than any man who bothered to put the time in. I wasn't stupid, I knew there had been rumors circulating my high school about me being gay because I never dated, never had sex with a boy. It only got marginally better when Dri and I graduated four years ago and started university, but I knew our small group of friends also wondered why I never dated or slept around.

And the truth is, nobody has excited me enough to want to have sex. I know that might sound pathetic to some, but I wasn't about to give up the goods just to scratch an itch. My pink rabbit vibrator took care of that itch just fine, thank you very much.

I wasn't holding out for Mr. Right either. I just wanted someone who lit up my body with one look, one touch. I wanted someone who could kiss me stupid. I wanted someone who would know what the hell they were doing! I was not going to settle for someone who was going to fumble around blindly with no freaking clue what a g-spot was.

Fellas, do us all a favor and google that shit. I've heard some horror stories from some of my other female friends about the one-night stands they took home. I just can't bring myself to have that memory for my first time, even though it's like some unspoken tradition that your first time is mostly fumbling around.

But this man, this man with my hand gripped securely in his, leading us away from the dance floor and over to a flight of stairs, this man whose name I still don't know is coming dangerously close to ticking off all my boxes.

Has my body reacting with one simple touch: check.

One look: check.

My eyes rake down the curve of his back to his ass and I have to hold back a groan when images of my nails digging into that ass while he pounds into me threaten to reduce me to a quivering mess.

"Like what you see?"

That groan slips past my lips when I lift my gaze and realize that he just caught me blatantly checking out his backside.

Heat creeps up my cheeks. "I'm sorry. I didn't mean…" I look away, embarrassed.

He unlocks an office door, motioning for me to go in first before he follows and closes the door behind us.

The owner obviously has very specific decorating tastes. The walls and floor match that of those downstairs, a big desk sits menacingly on the far side of the room, matching red curtains from the VIP rooms below hang in front of the two windows overlooking the rest of the club. It looks like something out of a Dracula movie.

"No need to be sorry," he whispers against my nape causing me to shiver from his closeness.

It's the second time he's managed to creep up behind me without a sound. Granted the music in the club is loud enough to drown out his footsteps, but up here it's virtually silent. Talk about soundproofing.

His one hand is back to curling around my hip while the other explores the curve of my spine before coming to rest against the opposite hip. Fingers curl into the fabric of my dress, pulling me flush against him, until there's nothing between us save for our clothes.

"I thought you wanted to get a refill of your drink?" I try, unsuccessfully, to mask the slight pant in my voice. Despite the clothes separating our bodies, I can still feel every hard inch of his chest, and when he subtly thrusts his hips forward, I can feel every hard inch of him there, too. Every. Hard. Inch.

"I'm working on it, Mia Bella, but it's not alcohol I'm after." He runs his nose down my neck, and nips at the curve where my neck meets my shoulder.

"It's... It's not?"

"No."

"Then what are you after?"

The pads of his fingers dig further into my hips. I think I may have bruises tomorrow, but I could care less in this moment.

"You. This pussy."

It's just one word, but I felt the need, the desire behind it wash over me. My eyelids droop, my head tipping back to lean into his shoulder. His hands slid from their grip on my hips, one grazing up my ribs to cup my breast, the other sliding down over my belly to between my thighs.

"I-I don't even know your name."

He chuckles, his knee nudging my legs apart. "Don't worry, you'll be screaming it soon." He grips my chin between his thumb and forefinger, forcing me to look over my shoulder at him, then his lips crash down on mine.

There was nothing sweet about our first kiss. It was raw, hungry, bruising, and I wouldn't have wanted it any other way. The kiss was a lot like the man behind

15

it. It was a means to an end. The start of something explosive, only meant to be temporary but the effects lasting long after.

I knew this was only going to be a one-night stand. I wasn't expecting any grand gesture of love after only one night of meeting, but somewhere, somehow, I knew that after tonight I would leave here craving more of him. A more that I knew he never would be able to give. This man oozed wealth and power, and there was a darkness surrounding him that I assumed he wore as a cloak. He hid behind it. It warned people away from him. Why? I wasn't sure, and I was never going to find out.

His tongue found mine, curling around it and sucking it into his mouth. I moan, reaching back and winding my hand around his nape, holding him in place and praying that he never stopped what he was doing. He nips my bottom lip, my mouth following his when he leans back.

"I don't do sweet and gentle, Mia Bella. Need to know if this is what you want. Need to be balls deep inside you, feel you tight around me."

I swallow hard, heat creeping back up my cheeks. I was hoping we would be further along before I had to tell him I've never done this before. Warm hands grip my hips, spinning me to face him. He uses his big body to back me further into the room until my ass hits the cold of the desk.

"Don't read minds, Mia Bella. Need to hear the words." His nose is back to doing that thing along my neck, like he's trying to ingrain the way I smell into his memory.

16

The palms of his hands now resting on the globes of my ass, and every inch of his front is pressed into mine. The length of his hard cock pressed against my stomach, I can feel it twitch, and I'd be damned if that didn't make my core clench tighter. Wetness pooled in my barely-there panties.

"I, um, I've never—"

I don't get very far with my explanation when the door suddenly flies open. A giant of a man silhouetted by the lights of the club downstairs stands in the doorway.

"Boss, we have a problem," the giant says in a fading accent.

"Dammit, Alessandro, can't you see I'm a little busy?" He barks at the intruder, but doesn't stop his active perusal of my body. A tongue licks up my collarbone just as his hands lift me under my backside and sit me down on the edge of the desk, his big body following and situating himself exactly where both of us need him to be.

"It can't wait, Boss."

"Fuck," he roars, leaning his forehead down to rest between the tops of my breasts, his breath sending more shivers down my body. After a few beats, his dark eyes slide up to capture my pale blues, longing and desire behind his. "Sorry, babe, but business is business."

He takes my hand, helping me readjust my dress, although his hands linger a little too long under the curve of my ass, before walking me back downstairs. When we reach the bottom step he stops suddenly, catching me off guard, and then pulls me into him. His hands on either side of my neck. It's the second time he's kissed me like this, and I wish it wasn't the last. My fingers curl into the front of his dress shirt as I hold him to me and try to deepen the kiss.

"De Luca," he says against my lips.

"Hm?"

"My name, Mia Bella. Braxton De Luca." His lips press against mine again, but for a peck this time, before he pulls away and turns to go out a set of steel doors I hadn't noticed until now.

"Braxton." I try out his name on my swollen lips. Unsurprisingly liking the way it feels on my tongue.

Kiss me stupid: check.

THREE

BRAXTON

"**P**LEASE, MR. DE Luca," the man sitting on the other side of my desk pleads. His suit is wrinkled, dark circles outline his eyes which I'm assuming is from the stress and lack of sleep plaguing him since finding out at the bank is repossessing his house the same week as finding out his youngest daughter has cancer.

My eyes quickly scan the paperwork in front of me. There is no doubt that the money he's asking me to lend him would go a long way in providing for his family while covering all of his daughter's medical bills and preventing the bank from repossessing the moderate house on the outskirts of the city. There is also very little doubt that if I agree to help him out, he will not be able to pay back his debt in the required time frame.

I raise my gaze from the papers sprawled in front of me and meet his at the same time Gio pushes open the door to the office and silently makes his way to stand behind the man.

"Mr. Michaels - "

"Mr De Luca," he interrupts, his shoulders hunching forward making me look like he's folding in on himself. "I'll do whatever I have to to pay it all back. And if I can't..." he pauses, taking a deep breath. "Well, if I can't then...then you can kill me. It'll be worth it, knowing my daughter got the treatment she deserves."

I look over my right shoulder at Alessandro and he gives me a clipped nod. When I look back to Gio, he nods too.

"Okay, Mr. Michaels, I'll loan you the money you need." Leaning my elbows on the desk, I fold one hand over the other and lean forward, making sure I have his full attention before I continue. "But you won't be paying with your life. Well, not in the way you think. If you cannot pay back the loan, which I suspect will be the case, then you will be become an associate for the famiglia."

"What..." he swallows hard. "What does that mean."

"It means if the Mafia needs you to do something, you do it. No questions asked," Alessandro says.

Michaels looks from me to Alessandro and back to me. "But my daughter will get the treatment she needs?"

"She will."

He doesn't seem to think very long about it before sitting up straighter, wiping his palms down his suit pants before nodding. "Deal."

I sign the papers authorizing the bank to transfer the exact amount into his bank account then push away from the desk, rebuttoning my suit jacket when I stand. Michaels shakes hands with me before Gio is escorting him out of the office, before they cross over the threshold, I stop him.

"Mr. Michaels, if you run I will find you, and you don't want me to come after you. Understand?"

His Adam's apple bobs and he looks like he wants to say something but thinks better of it, turning and allowing Gio to escort him from the building.

My computer pings with an incoming email. I'm a little surprised when I retake my seat behind my desk and open it, revealing the information I requested just this morning. All thoughts of Judge Michaels vanish and I immediately start coming up with a plan on how I can run into her again.

***

(Klara)

"Where did you disappear to last night?" Adrienne questions when I sidle up next to her at the breakfast bar the next morning.

After Braxton left me at the bottom of the stairs last night, I couldn't stop thinking about what happened in that office. I knew Dri would be fine at the club without me after I had spotted two of our other friends and Matt with her on the dance floor, so I made a beeline for the front door and called a cab.

No sooner had I closed the front door and kicked off my shoes was my rabbit vibrator being pulled out of its storage spot in the top drawer of my dresser. Let's just say that it got quite the workout last night. Even still, it didn't help ease the ache that now existed between my legs. I knew nothing would, except for Braxton De Luca.

"Decided to call it an early night when the alcohol started mixing with the cold meds. Wasn't keen on ending up face down in a dark corner somewhere." I was only half lying. I knew if the night had continued the way it was then I would've ended up face down... just face down with Braxton's hard cock pounding into me from behind.

Aaand that's enough of that train of thought.

I don't know why I lied to my best friend. If anyone knows about one-night stands it would be her. Or um, almost one-night stand? But how would I even begin to explain to her what happened? Some tall, dark, and sexy-as-sin man came up to me on the dance floor, started putting his hands on me, and asked if I wanted a refill. When I said no he gripped my hand and led me away to a dark office upstairs where he kissed me silly, and if we hadn't been rudely interrupted I would've given him my virginity against that sleek, black desk. Oh, and let's not forget that through all of this I didn't known his name. No, that piece of information was reserved for after he dropped me back off downstairs.

I inwardly groan, resting my head against the hand propped up on the breakfast bar. The aroma of fresh coffee and sizzling bacon permeating the air around me. Dri slides off her stool when the coffeemaker chimes signalling it's ready. Her white tank top riding up her toned stomach when she reaches above her to pull down two mugs for us.

I was slightly envious of my best friend. She had the type of body men drooled over. She was slim and toned, her boobs weren't too big, and her ass wasn't huge. Her skin was flawless, her hair a natural mahogany brown. Everything about her was just effortless. She didn't have to spend countless hours working out at the gym, or watching what she ate. She looked freaking gorgeous with her hair thrown into a high ponytail, workout leggings and a tank top—sans bra.

My eyes drop to my own triple d's and I sigh, taking in the bra I threw on before walking out of my bedroom this morning. I know I could've just left it off, after all, it was just Dri in the apartment, but there was always a part of me that was... not scared, but wary? Of going without one. Compared to Adrienne I was a bit on the bigger side. I wasn't overweight, actually far from it. But I had curves, very noticeable curves. It took me a helluva long time to come to terms with the fact that no matter how much I worked out or starved myself in the past, there was no changing my body shape. So, instead of trying to cover it with baggy clothes, I figured out how to start loving the way I look. I'm finally starting to get to the point where I can wear the dresses I want, and wear them with confidence. Plus, the way Braxton couldn't keep his hands off me last night proved that I looked hella good in the red dress, too.

Once we're done eating I help Dri load the dishwasher and clean the kitchen while she tells me about her plans for the weekend. I know I should be paying attention, but my mind's elsewhere. Disappointment pangs behind my chest when I realize I may never find out what would've happened if we hadn't been rudely interrupted in that office, but more than that, I realize I'm disappointed I may never get to see Braxton De Luca again.

***

After Adrienne left to take care of her errands I decide that I'm not going to sit around the apartment wondering about what if's. Stuffing my laptop and textbooks into my oversized purse I resolve to take advantage of the crisp, early spring air and walk to the café down the street from our apartment. I loved the big city. Where some people love how small they feel standing on a beach at the edge of an ocean, the city is like my ocean. I love that I can get lost easily in the throne of people. I love the busyness, the fact that nobody knows anybody's business. I love how small being in the heart of the city makes me feel.

"Good morning, Klara." Jen, one of the baristas, greets me cheerily when I push through the door.

"Hey Jen," I pause, dropping my bag at my favorite table on the side of windows racing parallel to the street, facing the door of the café. I like people watching whenever my brain gets too overloaded with information on my grad paper and I have to take a break. This is the perfect spot for me to indulge, while also indulging in my favorite coffee.

"Let me guess, white mocha americano misto?" Jen giggles when I make my way up to the counter.

I laugh. "I'm that predictable, huh?"

She shrugs, writing my name on the cardboard sleeve. "Hey, if it ain't broke don't fix it, right?"

"Right." I grin, and get a whiff of something that instantly makes my mouth water, giving me insight into who did the baking for the café that morning. "Your mom made double chocolate brownies?" I ask, bouncing on the balls of my feet like a giddy child.

"She did." Jen laughs. "She also made sure that I set one aside for you and put your name on it."

Jen hands me the coffee mug as well as a paper bag and I'm pretty sure my morning couldn't get any better, but I'm wrong because as soon as I turn around to go back to my table I lock eyes with a very familiar pair of dark ones. Ones that burned with heat as his fingers trailed up my thigh last night in the darkened room above the club.

Braxton De Luca stands before me with a casual hand in his dress pants and an easy smirk on his handsome face.

"It's you." My fingers tighten around the paper cup in fear that I may drop it and spill precious espresso goodness everywhere, but also because I'm trying my damn hardest not to drool.

The early morning sun illuminates him from behind, accentuating his tan skin and dark hair. I realize that this is the first time I'm really seeing him. I couldn't get a good look with the low lights of the club, but here in this café, nothing is obstructing my view.

"It's me." He chuckles, dark midnight eyes taking me in from head to toe, lingering a little longer on my chest.

Ah, so he's a boob man. That's… good to know.

"Wh-What are you doing here?" I stammer.

"I was in the neighborhood and heard this place as the best coffee on the block." He pauses, his smirk growing as he eyes me. "Care to join me for a coffee, Mia Bella?"

I hadn't picked up on it last night because I was... well, distracted, but his voice has a slight Italian accent. Like maybe he was born there but immigrated when he was young. I make a mental note to ask him about it later. Assuming there is a later.

"I-I can't. I have a paper to finish writing. I'm sorry."

My heart and my brain are at war with each other. My heart telling me to shut up and take it back. Of course, we'd love to have coffee with you. My body agreeing. But my brain, the more responsible one out of the three, is kindly reminding me that I have less than three weeks to finish this paper before I have to present it and then graduation. After which I'd officially be a doctor... of psychology, but a doctor, nonetheless.

Seeing Braxton standing in front of me, looking hot as all get out in his designer suit with his dark hair slicked back, is making me want to throw caution to the wind and tell my brain to take a hike. Especially when he lifts a hand and runs a thumb over his bottom lip. Dear god, that lip! Memories of wanting to suck on that lip flash through my mind. My core clenches.

"If you change your mind I'll just be over there." He hooks a thumb over his shoulder at the table directly across from mine and I have to swallow back a groan.

If I thought it was going to be hard trying to concentrate with him in the same room, then it was going to be damn near impossible with him sitting directly across the room with his table facing mine. It's then that I realize he gave me his name but I never gave him mine.

"It's Klara by the way. Klara Blouin." I grin and make my way over to my table. Butterflies take flight in my belly when I overhear him repeat my name.

"Klara."

I briefly wonder what it would sound like leaving his tongue while he orgasms, his body crushing me beneath its weight. Then I shut the door on those thoughts and get to work on writing this paper.

An hour in and all I've done is stare at the blinking cursor, watching as it mocks me. I take in a deep breath and exhale it through my mouth knowing that I'm going to end up sitting with him and this paper isn't going to get written…at least not while I can feel his eyes on me from across the café.

I tried. I tried so hard to ignore the intense heat of his gaze, but I was weak and found myself involuntarily shooting quick glances out the corner of my eye to see what he was doing. The first time I looked over I was shocked to see him with his nose in a book. That skyrocketed my attraction to him up another notch…or two. To me there was nothing hotter than a man who enjoyed reading, well, maybe a man in a tailored suit. Sensing someone watching him, he glanced up at me over the top of the book and grinned, sending those damn butterflies loose in my belly again.

The second time I glanced over it looked like he was in a heated phone conversation with someone. He looked stressed, leaning over with his elbows braced on his knees, a hand running through his slicked back hair. I gripped the ends of the table, having to physically stop myself from going over there and seeing if he was okay, from sliding onto his lap and kissing up that thick neck in hopes of taking his mind off whatever it was that got him so worked up. He never looked up to catch my gaze that time. I was silently grateful because it allowed me time to really take him in.

Every time I peeked over after that he was watching me. I sigh, closing the lid of my laptop, and secretly wonder what he did if he just happened to be able to spend the day in a café watching me.

Braxton quirks an eyebrow when I take the seat across from him.

"Done already?"

I finger the hair tie around my wrist. It's something I've been subconsciously doing ever since I was little. Whenever I was nervous or feeling a little anxious I would run my finger under the hair tie and spin it around my wrist. I didn't do it as often anymore because I had my gravity blanket now, but I couldn't exactly carry that around with me wherever I went. So, the hair tie acted as my travel-sized gravity blanket. "No, I decided to call it a day."

"Must've gotten a lot done in an hour to already be calling it a day, Mia Bella." The corner of his mouth tipped up into a knowing smirk.

I shrug. "I was a bit distracted. Couldn't concentrate."

I look at him pointedly, but that half smirk turns into a full grin, as if he knows exactly what he does to me.

"I see." That damn thumb is back to running across that bottom lip. It's like a magnet, always drawing my eyes in, with a direct line to my pussy.

"Does that mean the rest of your day is free to spend with me?"

"Um, like a date?" I ask, shifting nervously in my seat.

His eyes darken, his features going cold. "I don't date, Mia Bella. But you… there's something about you that makes me want to forget everything I know." He looks away and swallows hard before turning those intense eyes back on me. I want to ask him what he means by that. Why would I make him want to forget everything he knows? I want to know what secrets lie within his heart.

"Will you spend the day with me, Klara?"

No, my brain screams.

Yes, my heart screams back.

Fuck yes, my body screams in agreement. My nipples hardening beneath my thin sweater at the sound of my name on his tongue again.

"Okay." I nod. I would do the responsible grad student thing tomorrow, but today… today I was going to throw caution to the wind, tell my brain to shut up, and enjoy the here and now. I haven't been able to get Braxton out of my head since last night; his touch, his smell, the feel of his hard body pressed against me, all of it was a heady combination.

As much as I want to see where this thing goes, part of me knows I'll never be the same after Braxton leaves, because he will leave. He as much as told me that himself. Braxton was going to break me, and maybe I was just stupid enough to let him.

FOUR

"TELL ME, WHAT'S your paper on, Mia Bella?"

The city disappears around us as Braxton zooms up Austin Terrace. After we left the café earlier this morning he asked me what my favourite things to do around the city were, and then he made us do them. The Hockey Hall of Fame, shopping at Eaton Centre, walking through Union Station.

I always used to think the station looked like a miniature Grand Central station, but I had never been to New York so I could be completely off base with how similar they are. But Union Station and Eaton Centre were connected by an underground walkway. He wanted to drive us to the shopping centre, and I insisted that I wanted to walk through the underground pathway. I told him he could drive if he wanted to but I was going to walk it. He eventually caved, slipping his hand through mine, not letting go even after we made it through to the other side.

There was nothing extravagant about our day, it wasn't the typical romantic date and I was surprisingly okay with that. I was more than okay with it. This date, spending the day with Braxton exploring the city the way I loved, was better than any romantic date I have been on.

His hand squeezes my knee and I realize I've been so deep in thought about our day that I never answered his question.

"It's um... it's about the connection between mental health, diet, and exercise." My cheeks heat and I turn to look out the window, knowing the question that usually follows when I tell someone about the topic of my grad paper. It was the same subject I chose to do my thesis on when I was an undergrad, but now I was able to spend more time on the research and expand on it.

What made you decide on that particular subject? I can see how the rest of the night will go. He'll ask what made me choose that particular subject, and because I can't lie, I'll tell him it's because I struggle with mental illness on a regular basis. He'll look shocked, but try to play it off like it doesn't bother him, but I'll see in his eyes that it does. He won't end the day though, he'll politely continue whatever he has planned and then take me home. He won't come in either, and he won't call or text.

I hold my breath, waiting. I close my eyes wishing—not for the first time—that I was normal. That I didn't have this daily struggle going on inside me. But I'm not normal, and I do struggle on a daily basis. It's not that I'm ashamed of my disease. It's that I hate the sympathetic looks people give me when they find out I have anxiety and depression.

I have a disease, but I am not my disease. I am stronger than it, and I refuse to let it win. I refuse to be another statistic in a textbook. Do I have my bad days? Fucking right, I do. But I don't let one day dictate the rest.

Braxton is quiet when he pulls up to the gates of castle Casa Loma. The grounds look like they've been closed for a while, and when I chance a glance at the dashboard in the car I see that the grounds should've been closed to the public almost two hours ago. A guard runs out and opens the gates, ushering us through. I want to question him about it, but then the castle comes into view and words fail to form.

The castle sits against the backdrop of a newly darkened sky, spotlights on the ground are focused up on the castle, causing it to almost...glow? There's a light in the fountain in the centre of the drive, illuminating the water.

He parks the sleek black coupe. Stepping out and walking around the front of the car to open my door. I'm suddenly more nervous and anxious around him now than I've been all day. It doesn't make sense, but then again, it does. He never responded when I told him the topic of my paper, of what I've worked the last six years towards—four years of undergrad and getting my bachelors, followed by a combined two year program that'll award me both my Masters and my PhD in a few short weeks. I realize that I so desperately want him to be different, and if he's going to play the polite gentleman only to leave me wondering what I did wrong later then I'd much rather skip the charade and call it a night right now. I'd much rather go home and Netflix and chill by myself than spend more time with him wondering what's so wrong with me that he can't look past my anxiety.

Braxton reaches a hand out for me to take but I hesitate. Do I want to put myself through this? Can I really sit through another few hours of being around him?

"Mia Bella? Our dinner is waiting." He stands with his hand still outstretched, waiting for me to accept it and step out of the car but I just can't. "Klara?" There's a hint of concern marring his voice but I can't force myself to look up at him right now. I'm having a hard-enough time breathing. My vision is blurring and I feel like I'm going to pass out at any moment.

I hear Braxton curse before he's gripping my hips and turning me in the seat to face him as he kneels down in front of me, face to face. His hand wraps around my nape and he forces my head down between my knees. "Breathe, Klara. Just breathe for me."

I want to tell him that I can't. That it's too hard, it feels like there's a weight pushing down on my chest, and no matter how hard I try to get it off it just won't budge. Braxton keeps talking to me, his voice low and soothing as he whispers in my ear, his breath tickling the side of my face.

"Focus on my voice, Mia Bella. Focus on me, nothing else, and just breathe."

It's getting a little easier. The weight becoming lighter and lighter with every word that he whispers. When he senses that I'm okay, Braxton places a soft kiss on my forehead, his lips lingering against my heated flesh.

"I-I'm sorry." I'm about to ask him to just take me home but the next words out of his mouth have me stopping.

"It's okay, Klara. It's not my first rodeo."

"What—"

"Come," he takes my hand in his, closing the car door behind me and setting the alarm. "I'm starving, and I know you must be, too."

"Why...What..." My mind is racing with so many questions. What did he mean it wasn't his first rodeo? How did he know exactly what to do to stop my attack?

He places a hand on my lower back, urging me up the front stairs and through the entrance. Casa Loma has been one of my favorite places in this city ever since I discovered it back in high school. I love doing the guided tour and finding out who used to live here. It's usually always full of tourists walking around, but tonight there's no one here except for us.

Braxton steers us down the hallway to the left. We pass by the library, which is one of my favorite rooms in the castle, and then the dining room. I frown when we walk by, sure he said we were having dinner here. But then we enter the conservatory and I stop breathing. The only light coming from the candles on the lone table in the middle of the room, and the moonlight shining down from the stained-glass skylight.

Once we're seated the waiter arrives with our meals covered by a metal dome, and places a plate down in from each of us. When he lifts the lid, I'm expecting a glamorous meal but what appears on the plate is...a slice of pizza. I can't help the laugh that bubbles out. Once I get a handle on myself I glance up at Braxton, worried that I may have embarrassed myself again with my outburst. But he's just sitting there, staring at me. Something flashes in his eyes but then it's gone as a smile pulls at his lips.

"Had to leave something for the second date. Couldn't do all the romantic on the first." He raises an eyebrow at the pizza as if asking for my approval.

"Pizza is perfect. Thank you."

The rest of dinner goes by in a blur. I tell him about my family, about Adrienne, and he asks more questions about school and what my plans are for after graduation next month. He tells me about his family, that yes, his family is from Italy. Sicily to be exact. He talks about his best friend since childhood, Antonio, who also moved here with his family around the same time Braxton's did. And that he thought his parents must've thought they were funny giving him an English first name when the rest of the family all had Italian first and last names. When I ask him about what he does for work, his answer is a little more clipped, less forthcoming.

"Finances. I work a lot in investments," was the only answer I got before he switched the conversation back to me.

***

It's late by the time we pull up in front of the apartment I share with Dri. I'm tired but I don't want this day to end yet. I've had fun with Braxton, and I guess a part of me is scared that once I step out of this car and close the door that'll be it. I have no idea how to get a hold of him, or even where he works.

He surprises me again when he rounds the car to open my door, helping me out, then proceeding to walk me to my door. Braxton turns me around and pushes me back into my apartment door before I can get my key out to unlock it. His lips find mine, his tongue running along the seam, silently coaxing me to open for him. I moan when I do and his tongue slides in, finding mine.

"You make me lose my mind, Klara. Make me want to lose control." He presses soft kisses to the corner of my mouth and along my jaw to that secret spot behind my ear. "Losing control is dangerous in my life, but you're like a drug, Mia Bella. A drug I can't seem to walk away from."

Fingers skim down my sides, around my hip and over my ass, making me arch into him. Braxton growls when I rub against him, his lips seeking out mine again.

Somewhere in the distance my brain registers the sound of a ringing phone, but all I can concentrate on in this moment is Braxton's lips working against mine, his strong arms wrapping around me.

The ringing stops and starts again not even a second later. Braxton curses, his eyes pained when he pulls away from me and reaches into the pocket of his dress pants to retrieve the culprit.

"De Luca," he barks.

I should give him his privacy and turn around to unlock the apartment door, but I don't. Instead, my fingers find the button on his suit jacket and undo them before I can reach for the buttons on his dress shirt, his hand wraps around my wrist, halting my progress.

"I have to go, Klara."

"Oh. Okay," I gulp, turning around and praying my hand doesn't shake as I reach out and slide the key in the lock.

Before I can open the door, I feel him behind me. A hand sweeps my long hair off my shoulder, his breath warm against the nape of my neck. "'Til next time, beautiful," he says, placing a soft kiss on my shoulder and then he's gone.

***

Sundays have always been my do-nothing days. The days where Dri and I stay in our pajamas and spend the day either catching up on shows we missed throughout the week or indulging in a movie marathon. Sometimes it entails me getting lost in the newest book I downloaded on my kindle while Dri catches up on her reality tv shows. I can't stand those shows. They're so overdone, and have they ever actually been 'reality'? I feel like a good percentage of them are all scripted. And the drama isn't my thing either. Although, I must admit that my one guilty pleasure was Total Divas... for like the first season.

But today is different. Today, I can't seem to focus on the book currently pulled up on my kindle, my mind instead choosing to drift to Braxton and what he's doing today and the kiss we shared in the hallway. I find myself wanting to know things about him I shouldn't. Like, how does he take his coffee, or is he more of a tea guy? What does he do on his days off? What music does he listen to? Does he prefer summer or winter in the city? Does he even like the city, or is he more of a country man?

I giggle then instantly slap my hand over my mouth and look over at Dri in slight horror but her full attention is still on the tv. I slump back further into my side of the couch, relieved that she didn't hear my slip.

There's no way that Braxton prefers the country over the city. I can't even imagine him, in his tailored, designer suits sitting on a porch swing of a farmhouse, surrounded by nothing but open land. The two just don't mesh together. The idea of open land, no one for miles, is appealing. No one to hear me scream while Braxton pounds into me from behind, my hair wrapped around his fist, my back arched just for him.

I jump up from my spot on the couch, sending my kindle falling to the carpet. My cheeks heat as Dri glances up at me, concern written on her face.

"I, um," I clear my throat. "I'm going to get coffee. You want anything?"

"You okay?" Dri asks, quirking an eyebrow.

"Fine. Just need a caffeine pick me up." I paste on a smile, hoping she doesn't sense my unease. She doesn't.

I'm dressed in skinny jeans, my favorite pair of Vans, and a tank top and bounding down the stairs of our building less than five minutes later. As I push open the heavy glass door, a dark figure leaning against the brick wall catches my attention.

My breath hitches, my heart sputtering to a stop before kick starting just as the figure starts walking toward me, a cigar dangling between the fingers of his right hand.

"What are you doing here?"

The back of his hand runs down the side of my face, his dark eyes taking in the tank top that doesn't do a good job concealing the tops of my breasts, down to the blue Vans.

"Came to see you, Mia Bella."

"Your idea of seeing me is waiting on the sidewalk, hoping I'll come down?" I grin.

"I was about to call you to come down."

"How do you know my number? I don't remember giving it to you."

Braxton grins, his thumb running over my lips, his eyes heating. "I know a lot of things, Mia Bella."

"Like what?" I ask, almost panting, the sweet smell of cigar smoke tickling my nose.

He drops his hand, taking a step back and shaking his head. "Come," he says, holding out his elbow for me to take. "Let's take a walk. Grab a coffee," he adds when he senses my hesitation.

Braxton pays for my Americano Misto—against my protests—and his black coffee. I should've figured he was a black coffee kinda guy. We make it to the park by the university before either one of us speaks again. It's a comfortable silence, don't get me wrong, but I'm itching to learn more about him. To learn more about the man under the suit, under the persona.

"I had a good time last night. Thank you." I try to rack my brain for something more to say, but when I'm around him something happens between my brain and my mouth, and it's like all connection is lost. I know what I want to ask him, to tell him, but I have no idea how or even where to start.

He chuckles, leading us to a bench. "You're welcome, Mia Bella."

I take a seat, cocking my head to the side. "What does that mean? You've called me that quite a bit."

Braxton grins, taking the seat next to me. "It means my beautiful."

He glances at me out the corner of his eye, waiting to see my reaction, but all I can do is sit and stare at him, sure my jaw is resting on the floor with his admission. There's no way Braxton thinks I'm beautiful. I mean, look at him. He even looks important just sitting on a park bench with a coffee cup in his hand. His dark hair is slicked back again, not a hair out of place, and my fingers itch to run through it, to see what he looks like when he's not so perfectly put together. I want to see what he looks like when he first wakes up in the morning, when his voice is filled with sleep.

I take a sip of my coffee and try to swallow past the lump in my throat. "How did you know what to do that night in your car?" I don't know where that question came from. That part of the night is the furthest thing from my mind at his moment, but something he said to me after that has been nagging at me, I guess.

"My sister," he clears his throat, his gaze trained on a tree in the distance.

"She had panic attacks?"

"Panic attacks, anxiety, severe depression." His jaw ticks. "The panic attacks were usually always a result of the anxiety. She would work herself up so much that it would cause a panic attack." He hunches forward, leaning his elbows on his knees and placing his coffee cup on the ground between his feet. "We didn't know how bad the depression was until it was too late."

I don't know what the appropriate thing is to say to him. I'm sorry doesn't seem like it'll cut it. So I don't say anything, choosing to stay quiet in hopes that he'll continue.

"She was always so good at hiding her emotions. She had to be, growing up with the father we did. I was the only one in the family who knew about her anxiety, and that was only because I happened to walk in mid attack. She was embarrassed that I had seen it, and she hated the fact that I had watched it happen. Always so prideful. So stubborn. She refused any help I offered. Insisted that it was her burden to bear, and that she was handling it."

His shoulders deflate, and I think this is the first time I'm seeing him without a mask in place. This isn't some dark persona to keep people away. This is the real Braxton. I lay a hand on his shoulder, but that causes him to stiffen almost immediately, and I regret my decision to do it.

"Do you mind me asking what happened?"

He hangs his head and I'm sure he's not going to tell me. Heck, I wouldn't tell me either. We don't know each other very well and this is some heavy shit.

"I found her in the bathtub the day before her eighteenth birthday." He blows out a harsh breath before continuing. "She had slit both her wrists."

"Oh, Braxton—"

"The EMT's said she had been gone for a while before I found her. I was at a fucking business meeting with my father when my sister was taking her own life."

"I'm so sorry," I whisper, pulling him into me and wrapping my arms around his broad shoulders. I know those three little words offer no comfort but I don't know what else to tell him right now that will, So I do the only thing I can think of and hold him.

It seems like minutes, but I know it's only been seconds before I feel his full lips press against my neck

41

in a kiss. His fingers grip my hips, dragging me closer to him, until I'm almost sitting in his lap. Our coffees long forgotten.

"I need you, Mia Bella."

I swallow hard, my heart racing. "Okay," I breathe close to his ear at the same time my phone pings with a new message.

Dri: Gone to Matt's.

My palms are sweaty when I stand from the bench and pocket my phone. My throat is dry when I reach a hand out for Braxton to take, and those damn butterflies are fluttering in my belly again when I lead us back to my apartment.

FIVE

"**B**RAXTON...I-I'VE** never—" I swallow hard and try again, placing a hand on his solid chest. "I've never done this before. Sex. I've never..." My cheeks heat, and he stills his exploration of my body.

"Do you want me, Klara?" He slowly raises his head until we're face to face again. Dark, lust filled eyes meeting my hooded blues.

"Yes." As if to prove how much, I rub against him again, his cock twitching against my lower abdomen.

"Keys, Klara. Don't need an audience for what I'm about to do to you."

With shaking hands, I fumble around my oversized purse cursing myself the entire time. Why did I have to be drawn to the bigger, oversize purses? Why couldn't I be drawn to the cute shoulder ones, or the small clutches? 'Cause if I was then finding my keys would be a whole lot damn easier, and the sooner I find these damn keys, the faster I can get Braxton in my apartment, and finally get to see what lies beneath the expensive suits. Can finally feel his hard body against mine.

Finally, thank fuck, my fingers wrap around the cool metal and I unlock my door, stepping aside to let Braxton in. The minute he steps around me he has me pinned against the now closed front door. His hands back to their exploration of my body, his breath causing little wisps of my hair to tickle the back of my neck sending shivers racing down my spine.

Braxton abruptly spins me around, lifting me up causing my legs to wrap around his waist and pinning my back to the door. His teeth nip along my jaw before pulling my bottom lip into his mouth and sucking it. I moan, tightening my grip around his waist and pulling him closer. I can feel his rigid length rub against the wet spot coating my panties.

His fingers trail down my middle, dipping below the skirt of my dress. Braxton runs a finger up and down my satin covered slit. I moan and arch into his touch. It's not enough, I want more. I need more.

"Has anybody touched you like this, baby? You're already so wet for me, Mia Bella." His nose runs up my throat, nipping at my earlobe.

"No," I pant, trying to get closer.

His hands move from around my body, brushing the hair out of my eyes. Pinching my chin between his fingers he forces my face up to his. He's so close, if I were to lean forward an inch I could have his lips back on me.

"Good," he growls. "Once I have you, Klara, you're mine. No one else's. Understand? I don't share what's mine."

His hard eyes bore into mine expecting an answer. I don't give it a second thought. I nod and swallow hard, and try like hell not to dwell on his words too much. Not right now. Right now, I just need Braxton De Luca. All of him. Every single hard inch.

"I'm yours."

"Bedroom," he demands, nipping my bottom lip harder this time.

"It's the one on the left."

Our apartment is a simple open plan layout. When you walk through the front door, you walk immediately into the living room which leads directly into the open kitchen. There's a bedroom on either side of the apartment between the living room and kitchen. Dri's is on the right. We each have our own ensuite bathroom. The only thing that sucks about this building is the laundry room is in the basement, and is shared between all the units. But the rent is cheap-ish and I have my own bathroom so I can't really complain.

Braxton deposits me in the middle of the bed, immediately following me down, his hands sliding up my sides lifting my dress with them as they go until it slips past my fingers. His hands pin mine down into the soft sheets above my head, his nose buried in my neck again, his tongue licking a fiery trail up to my jaw. His fingers slide down my arms as he licks his way down my body, stopping to nip at the sensitive skin around my belly button, before continuing its trail down.

"Mmm, you smell as good as I remember, Mia Bella." Braxton runs his nose up my panty covered slit until his lips find my clit and he licks through the satin.

"Ahh," I moan, arching off the bed.

Braxton chuckles and does it again, obviously amused at my reaction. It's only when I buck my hips to try and get more friction he stops. His fingers curl around the waistband of my panties and sliding them down my legs.

"Tell me, Mia Bella, has anyone ever licked you here?" he asks, sliding a finger up and down my slit.

"N-No." I'm going out of my mind with need. I need him, his fingers, his lips, his cock. Him.

"Good." His warm breath skates over my exposed flesh. "Everything I kiss, everything my lips touch on this beautiful body is mine."

I barely have time to nod before I feel his tongue dart out and lick up my folds before finding my clit and flicking it. Once. Twice. Three times. Then his lips close around my clit and he sucks. Holy freaking shit! That feels so good.

Braxton slides a finger inside my pussy while his mouth works my clit. I'm not afraid to admit that I've given myself some pretty freaking great orgasms with my purple rabbit, but I can almost never come from just penetration alone. Ninety-percent of my orgasms have been clitoral. But I should've known that will never be a problem with Braxton because I can already feel it building inside me.

He sucks harder, his other hand reaching up to the undo the front clasp of my bra, immediately finding my nipple and pinching it between his fingers. I think I'm going to lose my mind. It's too much; his fingers tugging on my nipple, his lips around my clit, and now two fingers sliding in and out of my pussy. It's all too much, and I don't think I can take it anymore. Then he curls his fingers and I see stars. Braxton continues his onslaught through my orgasm, not stopping until the walls of my pussy stop clenching around his fingers.

He moves up my body, trailing little kisses along my hips, my stomach, between my breasts before circling each nipple with his tongue and drawing it into

46

his mouth, sucking until my back arches off the bed again, then continuing to trail those drugging kisses up my throat, along my jaw and finally, finally I get those lips back on mine.

He's marking me. Claiming me as his.

When my arms wrap around his back I realize that while I'm fully naked and exposed beneath him, Braxton is still fully dressed, but he doesn't protest when I work his dress shirt out of his pants, then my fingers are fumbling to undo the buttons and pushing the shirt off his shoulders.

My palms run over solid, sculptured muscle as I follow the smattering of neatly trimmed chest hair down between his pecs, over his abs, to the trail that disappears behind the waistband of his pants. Then he's moving away, standing at the foot of the bed. With heat blazing behind his lust-filled eyes, he undoes his belt, pushing his pants and boxers down legs as thick as tree trunks.

I gulp when my eyes land on his cock and the hand he has wrapped around it stroking slowly up and down. Up and down. All of a sudden, I feel as inexperienced as I am. I'm not sure I'll be able to take all of him. He's huge, and I'm a twenty-three-year-old virgin. Suddenly, this feels all wrong. He's so much more experienced than I am, he's also older by seven years—a fact I found out at dinner. Why would he want anything to do with me? I'm positive he could have his pick of women. Garnered by the all the looks he drew today, he would have no problem snapping his fingers and having an experienced woman at his feet, ready to do whatever he commanded. So why me?

Warm fingers wrap around my leg, lifting my foot before his lips are pressing a kiss to my inside ankle. Shivers race down my body, my core clenches. Fuck, that feels so good. With just one touch, I no longer care why I captured his attention. All I care about is that he's here now with me, and while it may never progress outside this room, I'm going to bask in his touch tonight.

I hear the tear of a foil wrapper seconds before Braxton is crawling back up my body, planting his elbows on either side of my head, his nose inches away from mine.

"Wrap your legs around my waist, Klara."

I do as he instructs and instantly feel him prodding at my entrance. My entire body stiffening. Braxton places soft kisses along my jaw.

"I'll go as slow as you want me to, Klara. You're in control here."

His words offer more comfort to me than he can ever know. With a shaky breath, I force my body to relax when I feel the head of his cock pushing in. The pain is instant. I have to shut my eyes and remind myself to not tense up, to keep breathing, but thankfully Braxton stills allowing me time to get used to his cock stretching me. Then after a while I start squirming beneath him, needing him to move.

Braxton kisses each one of my eyelids before resting his cheek against mine as he starts to move, slowly at first, and then his pace picks up when my hips buck up to meet each one of his downward thrusts. His scent wrapping around me like a security blanket.

I have no idea what the future holds for either one of us, but right here, right now, as I cling to Braxton De

Luca and my body races toward a free fall, I curse my heart for trying to attach itself to a man we cannot have. A man who only after one day already holds the potential to break my heart in ways I don't want to imagine. A man I know nothing about.

***

When I wake up the next morning I'm not surprised that Braxton is nowhere to be found. His side of the bed is already cold, telling me he probably waited until I fell asleep to sneak out. It shouldn't surprise me. I know it shouldn't. And yet, it still does. I'm not sure what I expected after last night.

That after I gave him a part of me nobody else has had he would magically want to stick around? Did I really expect that after one day he would want to be with me? Because if I did then I really am just a naïve little girl.

"Everything I kiss, everything my lips touch on this beautiful body is mine."

Was it all just lies to get me into bed?

I sigh, tossing an arm over my eyes. Get over it, Klara. He told you what he thought you wanted to hear to get you into bed. It was a one-night stand. Simple. You were practically begging for it.

Frustrated with the turn my thoughts have taken now that it's the day after, I throw back the covers and hop into a shower, allowing the hot warmth to ease away some of the ache in my muscles. I try to wash the smell of sex and Braxton from my body, but no matter how much I scrub, I can still feel his touch, still feel his

49

fingers gripping onto my hip, still feel his breath on my neck, his lips placing kisses behind my ear.

Knows what he's doing: Check.

Shutting the water off, I quickly dry off and throw on a clean pair of yoga pants and a racer back tank, tossing a sweater and change of clothes into my gym bag. The shower didn't help to get my mind off Braxton, it only added to the onslaught of images already playing, but maybe a session at the gym is just the thing I need.

Adrienne isn't out in the living room when I go to fill a shaker bottle with my usual pre-workout and water, and her door is still slightly ajar which likely means she never came home last night. My lips quirk in a half smile having some idea of where she likely spent last night.

I toss the gym bag over one shoulder so it's resting across my body making my way downstairs and out into the crisp early summer morning. I love days like this. When the morning still has that clean spring smell and feel to it, but by early afternoon it's hot and well on its way to being summer.

The gym is about a thirty-minute walk away, which gives me the perfect amount of time to drink my pre-workout and have it kick in by the time I hop on the elliptical. Usually, I'll do fifteen on the treadmill and fifteen on the elliptical as my warm up cardio, but today I need to sweat out some frustration. So as soon as I lock my bag in my locker, I jump on the elliptical, hit fast start and immediately try to get my stride up to 6.5.

It doesn't take long 'til I'm dripping sweat and my legs are burning. After wiping down the machine I move onto the leg press and stack forty-fives as well as thirty-fives on each side of the bar before climbing in and bracing my feet in a wide stance. I push up slightly and release the holds, then bring my knees down toward my chest before pushing back up. I do three sets of twenty-five of these before moving on to straight leg deadlifts. I do another three sets of twenty-five of these with a seventy-pound weighted bar. Leg and calf extensions are next before moving on to squats and finishing with straight leg kick backs. By the time I'm done an hour and a half has passed and I jump on the treadmill to finish out my workout with a moderate jog.

My fitness watch vibrates against my wrist letting me know that I reached my daily active minute goal already. Once my legs feel like jello and I feel like they can give out at any minute, I stop and wipe down the machine before marching off to the showers.

Two and a half hours after arriving at the gym, I push past the glass doors and make my way down to the subway station, hoping the train isn't late and I don't miss my first class of the week.

***

"Who is that, and why does he look like he wants to devour you whole, Klara?" Adrienne asks just as we sit down at one of the outside tables scattered around the university campus.

When I follow her line of sight and look over my shoulder, my eyes connect with Braxton's. That's because he already did, I want to answer, but don't.

Rick, another one of my best friends, glances over his shoulder before turning back to his burger, unimpressed. "That's Braxton De Luca. He's not someone you want to get involved with, Klara."

Dri and I both look at him, shocked. What does Rick know that I don't? Granted the list of things I do know is fucking minuscule, but still.

"And why's that?" Dri asks, an eyebrow raised.

Rick shrugs. "Just trust me. Stay away from him and the De Luca family. They're bad news." Rick drops his burger back into its wrapper before focusing his hazel eyes intently on me. "Promise me, Klara. Promise me you'll stay far away from that family."

Of course, I can't promise him that. No matter how much I want to assure my best friend that I'll stay away from Braxton, I can't. There's something about him that pulls me in every time he's near. Even now, my body is already responding to him even though he's not within touching distance.

"Why?" I lift my chin. "What makes them so bad?"

Rick shakes his head. "They're a dangerous family. Anyone associated with them has either shown up dead or is in jail for murder." He pauses, "At least that's what's been reported in the papers."

I want to reassure him that I know Braxton would never hurt me, but do I? I don't really know him that well, am I really that sure that he won't hurt me, not even accidentally?

Rick takes off after his phone rings, leaving Dri and I at the table by ourselves. I can still feel Braxton's eyes on my back as I will the food in my stomach to stay down.

"You know him, don't you?" Dri's dark eyes study me, like she's seeing through the calm façade I'm trying and failing at putting on.

I nod, pushing my salad around the plate with my fork, my appetite suddenly nonexistent.

"He's the guy you had in the apartment last night?"

Dri giggles when my eyes round in shock, my mouth opening and closing like a guppy. "I came home to grab a change of clothes and um... heard the noises coming from your bedroom."

"Oh god," I groan, dropping my fork on the plate and trying to disappear inside my denim jacket.

"That's what you said last night." She laughs.

"Not funny," I snap, throwing a blueberry at her but it misses and lands on the ground behind her.

Dri is still full out belly laughing when I feel him getting closer, sending a shiver down my back. His scent hitting me before I hear him stopping behind me. I slowly lift my eyes to Dri, who's staring in wide-eyed shock and appreciation at the specimen of a man standing behind me. She swallows hard, looking from him to me, him to me.

"I, uh," she clears her throat, "I'll um, see you in class, Klara." She rushes to gather her things and then scurries away.

I can feel his intense stare back on me but I refuse to turn around. I can handle him leaving in the middle of the night. I can handle that what we shared was probably a one-time thing, but what I cannot handle is him showing up at my school.

"Klara." He moves into my line of vision, taking up the seat Dri just vacated.

I take that as my cue to gather up my shit and leave without a word. I power walk, not sure where the hell I'm going since my next class is in the opposite direction. Then my eyes land and lock on the logo for the coffee store on campus, my feet automatically heading in that direction, my body knowing that copious amounts of coffee is the only way I'm going to survive today. Especially with my legs screaming at me to give them a damn break after the workout I put them through this morning.

Once I have my white mocha americano misto in hand, I breathe a little easier, sitting down in one of the wrought iron chairs outside the coffee shop. Seconds later, Braxton lowers his massive body into the one across of me. I should've known that he wouldn't allow me to brush him off that easy. Of-fucking-course not.

"I'm not good for you, Klara."

I scowl, not looking up at him, my eyes focusing on the lid of my coffee cup. "Then why are you here, Braxton?"

He pinches my chin between his thumb and forefinger, forcing my gaze up. "Because I owe you an explanation and I wanted you to see you one last time."

Wrenching my chin out of his grip, I stand, tossing my backpack over my shoulder. "Well, thanks for that, but it wasn't needed. I had a great time last night, and that's all it was. One night. I needed your help getting rid of a problem and you provided it. And you needed help forgetting. So, thank you. But now I'm late for class."

I storm off, trying like hell to not look back over my shoulder. I can feel his eyes tracking me until I push open the doors to the art building and they swing close behind me. For the first time since I laid eyes on him again, I can breathe a little easier, and then disappointment settles in. Disappointment that he never came after me. I shake it off and start the climb to the third-floor lecture rooms. I will not allow him to have this much power over me after just one damn night. It's bullshit.

I feel like a walking contradiction; wanting him to leave me alone but feeling disappointed when he didn't come after me. His admission that he's no good for me should not have this much effect on me. I should be able to just brush it off as a casual one-night. I should be grateful that he was honest with me and move on. So why do I want to know more about him, about his family, his life.

With a sigh, I pull open the door to the lecture room and find my seat, I don't have time to wonder about Braxton. I need to focus on my last month of school so that I can graduate and get the hell out of here. But as the professor begins his lecture, I don't hear a word coming from his mouth. No, all my thoughts are on the dark-haired man I left sitting at the campus café.

SIX

MY PRESENTATION COMES and goes, as well as final exams, and before I know it it's the start of summer vacation, and graduation is a little over a month away. My presentation went off without a hitch, and my supervisor said I had done an amazing job and would be surprised if I didn't have schools chomping at the bit to get me to teach. I was honored, and also a little overwhelmed. I had given teaching a thought but knew that's not where I ultimately want to end up. I want to help kids who struggle with mental illness on a daily basis. Kids who may not have had the support I did growing up. Kids like… Braxton's sister.

"Holy shit, Klara," Dri says, walking into my room, a whistle leaving her lips when she takes in my outfit for tonight.

Since today was the last day of final exams, I decided to say screw it and suggested to Dri that we go out. I also decided to take a chance and live a little which led to my buying this dress.

"If you're hoping to catch Braxton's attention tonight, then I'd say you picked the right outfit. He's not going to be able to keep his hands off you when he sees you." Dri sits down at my vanity and starts rummaging through my makeup.

"I'm not. And besides, I don't know if he'll be there again."

After that little thing with Braxton on campus, I came clean to Dri and told her about the night at the club. The first night I met Braxton De Luca. My gaze lands on my reflection in the mirror, my hands instantly flying to the fabric at my stomach and pulling it away from my body, watching as it settles against every one of my curves again. I try scrunching it in the middle and then pulling it taut again. Despite knowing how good I look in the dress, I still can't stop the automatic reaction every time I wear an article of clothing this revealing.

The black maxi-dress hugs my five-six body like a glove, accentuating the round curve of my ass and my breasts, the high slit making my legs look longer than they are, and the sleeveless top highlighting the fact that I work out. My ash-blonde hair is sitting atop my head in a messy bun with small sections framing my face in soft curls. My pale blue eyes are outlined in black making them more intense, my lips painted a dark berry. I know the dress isn't conducive to dancing, but I was more interested in getting my drink on than spending the entire night on the dance floor. I had to get my mind off Braxton, and since pushing myself past my limits at the gym wasn't helping, I was hoping a little rum or tequila would do the trick.

We hail a cab right outside our building, Dri giving the driver directions to the club while I settle against the leather seat and watch as the city rushes past us. Butterflies take flight in my belly at the thought of potentially running into Braxton. Despite my protests, I would give anything to feel his rough hands on my body again, to feel every hard inch of him pressed against me. To hear his voice, feel his breath against my heated skin. I squeeze my legs closed as my core clenches and my panties grow damp. No, dammit. Tonight is about trying to forget him, not remembering all the ways he made me scream his name.

Our cab pulls up to the warehouse and Dri pays the driver as I step out, waiting for her before approaching the bouncer. It's the same guy as last time, and he's no less menacing now than he was back then.

"Ready to get your party on?" Dri asks, sauntering over to me.

"Ready." I grin, looping my arm through hers when she proceeds to show the bouncer the business card and he opens the steel door, ushering us through.

The club is exactly how I remember it from the last time we were here. Only now my eyes are drawn to the set of hidden stairs in the far-right corner. The set of stairs that leads to an office, the same office that Braxton…

I shake my head and follow behind Dri as she pushes her way through the crowded dance floor. That's my best friend. Not giving a shit that she could've walked around the damn thing. She always finds the most direct route, and screw anyone who gets in her way. It's what drew me to her. She just doesn't give two fucks.

Adrienne orders us two porn star shots each, as well as a rum and Coke for me and a vodka cran for herself.

"To the end of our school career." She lifts the shot glass in a toast and we clink glasses before throwing the shot back. The alcohol leaving an overly sweet taste in my mouth. We do the second shot before grabbing our drinks from the bar and making our way over to a high-top table.

"Ready to dance?"

I tilt my head to the side, lifting my glass. "Need a few more of these first."

Dri laughs, already slipping back off the stool. "Watch my drink?" she asks, pushing her glass closer to mine and I nod, watching as every man in her path turns and gawks at her as she struts her way to the middle of the dance floor. That's right, struts! My best friend doesn't do anything half-assed.

"Didn't anyone ever tell you, you shouldn't mix alcohol, Mia Bella?"

My body stills at his voice. Braxton watches me from the seat Dri just vacated.

"Didn't anyone ever tell you not to sneak up on a lady?" I bite back.

He chuckles. "That they did. I apologize."

My eyebrows draw together as I take him in. Really take him in. He looks immaculate as always in a tailored, black, three-piece suit with a sapphire blue tie. But he looks…tired. Defeated. His eyes don't hold the same spark they did that day we explored the city, and there are bags forming underneath them. His jaw ticks under my scrutiny.

"What happened?" I'm not sure what prompted me to ask that question, but something deep in my gut is telling me that Braxton doesn't allow anyone to see him like this.

He glances at the dance floor, his Adams apple bobbing, his expression looking pained when he turns back to me. "You did," he whispers.

Screw him. I didn't ask for anything more than one fucking night, and technically, I never even asked for that either. He's the one who sought me out at the café, he's the one who suggested we spend the day together, he's the one who started what happened that night. And he's the one who left like a ghost in the middle of the night. "Well, I'm sorry I was such an inconvenience. It was one night, Braxton." My fingers tighten around mine and Dri's drinks as I move to stand from the table. Anger rolling through me.

"Klara," he sighs. "That's not what I meant."

"But it's what you said."

His hand grips my elbow, fingers tightening their hold. "Dammit, but it's not what I meant." He backs me into the nearest wall, sliding the glasses from my fingers and placing them on the table. "You fucking took me by surprise. I told you I don't date, Klara. Never had the desire to. Until you. I've never told anyone about my sister and yet I couldn't stop myself from telling you." He presses his palm over my racing heart. "I find myself wanting to be around you all the fucking time. Wanting to smell your scent on me. To feel that soft body arching beneath mine again." The tip of his nose trails up my throat, I'm quickly learning that this is his favorite thing to do while his hands roam my body. Like he's using all of his senses to imprint me onto his memory. "But I wasn't kidding when I said I'm no good for you. This life, Mia Bella, my life will destroy you."

I lift my chin, giving him better access to my neck. "I-I don't know what any of that means, Brax."

He stills, his mouth a hair's breadth away from the corner of my lips. "Say that again."

"Brax," I repeat.

His lips find mine in a bruising kiss, my arms wrapping around his shoulders, hands gripping the hair at his nape keeping him close to me.

"Nobody has ever given me a nickname. Fucking love hearing it come out of your mouth, Mia Bella."

I moan when his tongue pushes between my lips seeking out my own.

"I crave you, Klara. Even in my fucking dreams, my body craves your touch. But I can't be responsible for destroying your light, Mia Bella. Can't be the one who shrouds you in darkness. There's no more good left in me. Don't think there ever was."

"I believe there's good in you, Brax." I frame his face with my hands, forcing him to look into my eyes when I say those words, then I pepper his lips and his jaw with kisses.

"Baby, I'm the thing the monsters are afraid of," he warns.

I should heed his warning. Something deep in my gut is telling me to run as far as I can and never look back. To forget I ever heard the name Braxton De Luca, but I... can't. Because a bigger part of me is telling me to hold on with both hands, to wrap myself firmly around him and never let go, to show him that there is good in him.

"I don't care, Brax. You said your body craves my touch? Well mine craves yours just as much. I need you, Braxton. Tonight, tomorrow, however long I can have you. I want you."

His breath hitches, his eyes growing hooded. "You done with school?"

I nod.

"Good. Stay with me tonight, tomorrow. Fuck, stay the entire week, the entire month. Just wanna see you in my house, Mia Bella. Want to feel you in my bed."

"Okay."

***

I push through the bodies on the floor until I find Dri wrapped around a surfer wannabe. When I raise a questioning eyebrow and quickly glance from her to him and back again she giggles pressing her body further into his if that's even possible. By the giggle I can already tell she's halfway to drunk-ville and by the way she's wrapped around this dude, she'll probably be going home with him tonight which makes me wonder what happened with her and Matt.

"You okay?" I ask, chancing another glance at surfer dude.

"I'm fine," she slurs, but I can tell by her eyes she's not fine. She's hurting, and obviously using this poor dude to run from whatever it is that's causing the hurt.

"Dri, what happened with –" my words get cut off when I see Matt stalking through the crowd. His jaw set, eyes burning with possessiveness as he glances at where Dri is wrapped around the guy like a snake.

"Adrienne!" His voice booms over the music. I watch as my best friend visibly stills, her breath hitching as she slowly disentangles herself from surfer dude.

"Ready?" Braxton slips his arms around my middle, pressing his front to my back and nipping along my neck.

I look from Matt to Dri and back again. "You got this?" I ask Matt. He nods, eyes never leaving Adrienne.

There is not a guilt-ridden bone in my body when I turn and leave my best friend on the dance floor. I know she will be okay with Matt here now. Plus, it is about time she stops fighting whatever was happening between them and start admitting to some things. I glance out of the corner of my eye at Braxton as he drives us away from the club and toward his house, and inwardly sigh. Easier said than done.

SEVEN

MY JAW DROPS as black wrought iron gates open to a long road surrounded on either side by Catalpa trees, the white flowers already in full bloom, offering a country feel despite being just on the outskirts of the city. We continue up the drive for what feels like hours but must only have been minutes until a large house looms in front of us. A stone water feature in the middle of the circular driveway.

Braxton drives us right into one of four garages, motion sensor lights turning on as soon as the car enters, illuminating the entire garage. A black SUV, a motorcycle, and another sports car take up the other three bays. I do a double take at the motorcycle. It doesn't fit with the image I've seen of Braxton so far, and yet… it does.

"I thought you had a place in the city," I question, stepping around the hood of the car to join him.

"I do." He sets the alarm on the black coupe, placing a hand at the small of my back and ushering me forward. "I spend my weekends here and any lengthy amount of time I have off."

If I thought my jaw couldn't drop any lower, I was wrong—so wrong. Braxton ushers me through a door which leads us right into the kitchen. A pang of jealousy shoots through me as I take in the Italian inspired kitchen. A mix of granite countertops and wood cupboards, stainless steel appliances. It feels homey, and not at all what I expected Braxton's home to feel like.

I was expecting dark colors, and clean, sleek lines found in most modern furniture and homes. I was expecting his home to match the person he portrays to the world – cold and calculating. I was not expecting this.

Home. My brain screams, and I have to mentally shake the thought away.

Strong arms wrap around my waist, backing me into a countertop, fingers gripping my hips as Braxton lifts and sets me down on said countertop, stepping between my legs. The dress making it nearly impossible. A growl reverberates through his chest, his fingers pulling at the neckline until it rips all the way down, bearing my breasts to his gaze, and then my stomach. And finally, the rip meets the high slit and the dress falls away landing on the counter behind me.

I'm not even mad. I should be. I should be furious. That dress cost me almost a whole paycheck, but that… that was fucking hot, and as I make a mental note to wear something else that will make him lose control like that again, Braxton's hands find my bare hips, pulling me to the edge of the counter, his lips finding that sensitive spot below my ear that sends shivers down my spine every damn time.

"I need to feel you wrapped around me, Klara. Been too long, Mia Bella."

His one hand sprawls against my back holding me in place while his other dips behind my panties, his fingers finding my clit, starting a sensual rhythm. I moan, trying to get closer, trying to find the friction I need, the friction I crave from him.

In one swift move, Braxton tears through my panties leaving me in nothing but my bra. His fingers finding my hips again in a bruising grip.

"Going to take you hard and fast, Mia Bella. Need to feel this pussy gripping my cock."

I nod. Braxton lifts me from the counter and my legs instinctively wrap around his waist. He spins us, my back hitting the cold steel of the fridge hard, his hand undoing his belt and zipper one minute and the next he's pushing into me.

One hand supporting me under my ass, the other wrapped around my throat, Braxton pounds into me. His thrusts getting harder and faster as each minute ticks by. I'm not sure how much longer I can last like this. With every thrust his cock brushes my g-spot. The hand around my throat tightens a fraction, his lips capturing mine in a hard kiss. When his teeth sink into my bottom lip I can't hold back anymore, my pussy clenches so hard around him when I come that Braxton's thrusts falter for a second before they're back to their bruising pace. Several thrusts later, he grunts when he finds his own release. His hand falling away from my throat, his arms wrapping securely around me and carrying me to a nearby bathroom.

Braxton deposits me onto a bathroom counter. He steps away only long enough to turn the water on in the shower and get undressed. My body is so tired that I allow him to pick me up again and carry me into the shower with him. Braxton spends the next ten minutes washing every inch of my skin, paying careful attention to the area between my thighs. His fingers massaging my scalp as he washes my hair cause my lids to flutter closed, my body swaying under his gentle touch.

He rinses us both off, carrying me out of the shower stall again and gently standing me up on the soft bathroom floor mat. I watch under heavy lids as Braxton grabs a towel, lowers to his knees and starts drying me off, his lips following the path of the towel up my body. When they reach the apex of my thighs, he sucks on my clit until my legs begin to buckle under me. Steadying me with one hand he continues his lazy kisses up my stomach, sucking each nipple into his mouth, placing a kiss between my breasts, up my collarbone, at the curve of my neck, along my jaw. By the time he reaches my lips I feel high from all the attention he's showing my body.

Without a word, Braxton dries himself off then tosses the towel over the glass door of the shower, swoops me up and carries me into the joining bedroom. He doesn't let go of my body while he pulls the comforter down, lays us both on the bed and pulls the comforter back up over us, his hands gripping my hips again to pull my back snugly into his front cocooning me between his hard chest and his arm draped over me.

"Braxton –"

"I'm sorry, Klara," he says before I can get any words out. When I try to turn around, his arm tightens keeping me in place. "Sleep," he commands.

But sleep doesn't come. Instead I lie awake, staring into the dark room, wondering if he'll be gone again in the morning just like last time.

EIGHT

SLEEP MUST'VE COME for me sometime in the middle of the night because as I roll onto my back, warm sunlight streams through the floor to ceiling window, but the spot where Braxton slept last night is cold. Frustration and disappointment flood through me that I don't immediately notice the smell of coffee and bacon in the air.

Thinking Braxton may have gotten up earlier to make us breakfast has me jumping out of bed and shrugging into his dress shirt from last night. Padding out of the room still doing up the buttons, I don't immediately notice that it's not Braxton standing over the pan of sizzling bacon.

When I finally do lift my head, I'm greeted by a woman who must be in her early sixties. Hair as dark as Braxton's with streaks of grey frame a tanned face. But where Braxton's eyes are dark, hers are a deep blue.

"Ah, there you are. Braxton said not to wake you, but I thought you may be hungry once you awoke. Come, sit." She motions toward the breakfast bar and I take seat across from her, still not understanding who she is or why she's in his home. "Here," she says placing a heaping plate full of bacon, eggs, breakfast potatoes, and toast in front of me. "Eat. You're too thin," she tsks.

"Ma."

The sound of his voice coming from behind me startles me and I almost drop the fork I picked up a moment ago. When I crane my neck around, Braxton is leaning against the entryway to the kitchen, arms crossed over his chest, his feet crossed at his ankles, a small grin tugging at his full lips. Black dress pants slung low on his hips, a white dress shirt hanging open at his sides. I have to try really hard not to whimper at the sight of him.

"Don't Ma me," the woman admonishes, hands on her hips. "You told me not to wake her. I didn't wake her. Not my fault she can't resist the smell of my coffee any more than you can."

At the sound of coffee, I perk up trying to look over her shoulder to see where the coffeemaker's at, at the same time a big steaming mug is thrust in front of me. Braxton chuckles as I graciously thank his mom and accept the mug of caffeine goodness from her.

"I thought you had somewhere to be today, Ma." Braxton places a hand on my lower back as he claims the stool next to mine. His hand never leaving my body as he accepts his own coffee from his mother.

"Braxton De Luca, have you no manners? Aren't you going to introduce me to your girl?" She glares at him, quirking an eyebrow and causing me to almost choke on the hot liquid. Braxton makes the exact same facial expression when he challenges me.

Beside me, he sighs, running his hand up and down my back in a soothing gesture. Soothing me from what I have no idea. I'm loving this little interaction between him and his mother.

"Ma, this is Klara. Klara, this is my Ma."

"It's nice to meet you, Mrs. De Luca." I try extending a hand out for her to shake but she ignores it, instead coming around the breakfast bar to pull me into a crushing hug.

"Call me Ma. After all, it must be serious between you and my son if he's bringing you to this house."

"Ma," Braxton warns, but she ignores him, keeping her blue eyes trained on me.

"Be good to him, yeah?" Her eyes search mine and I swallow hard. "Don't hurt my boy," she adds only loud enough for me to hear, but words fail me. What do I even begin to say to that? That he has the potential to hurt me worse than I could him. That I'm already halfway in love with her son after only spending two days with him, and it has nothing to do with him being my first sexual partner, because I'm pretty sure I was halfway in love with him before we had sex. I do the only thing I can and nod.

She must approve of whatever she sees in my eyes because she pulls me in for another hug before stepping back and letting me go.

"Antonio is driving me to the airport," she says reaching for a suitcase I missed standing by the door to the garage.

"Ma, I told you I could've driven you." Braxton glares at his mother, his jaw ticking.

"Yes, and I told you that I didn't need you to drive me. Plus, you have company." She glances between us, a slow smile pulling at the corners of her lips.

Braxton sighs, running a hand through his disheveled hair and sliding off the stool to hug his mother. "Have fun in Sicily." He places a peck on her cheek and then she's gone.

With his full attention now on me I feel like running after her and telling her not to go. Heat blazes behind his eyes when he takes in the shirt I'm wearing. The dress shirt barely covers my thighs with the way I'm sitting on the barstool.

I gulp, watching the way his muscle tense with each stride he takes closer to me. His hands slip under the shirt, moving it up as his fingers inch up my thighs, my hips. Then he suddenly stops. Confused, I glance down. Small finger-shaped bruises decorate my hips from where his fingers dug into me last night.

"Braxton." My voice is barely above a whisper when he places his hands on either side of my face, moving my hair back from my nape. His brows furrow when he takes in the bruises along my throat, too.

He nuzzles into me, kissing the hollow of my neck. "I'm so fucking sorry, Klara. I should never have been so rough with you last night."

"W-What are you talking about?" I try to move back but he holds me in place.

"I should never have marked you like that. I'm so sorry. So fucking sorry."

"Don't." I shove him away but he's so strong, so solid that he doesn't waver. "I liked it, Braxton. I liked your fingers gripping my hips, leaving little marks. I liked your hand around my throat. I like knowing that you left your mark on me."

I can feel his head shaking but he still refuses to lift his head and meet my eyes.

"I. Liked. It," I reiterate. How does he not know this? He made me come so freaking hard I thought I was going to black out. I never thought I would like anything as rough as what we had done last night, but I did, and it just made me want him even more.

Braxton finally pulls himself away from the crook of my neck. My stomach falls from the look of pain on his face.

"Told you I'm no good for you, Mia Bella." He drops his hands, stepping away. His features going cold. "My driver will take you back to your apartment. Goodbye, Klara." His gaze rakes up me again like he's trying to remember everything about me. Braxton turns and I watch the way his muscles move at his back until he walks into what must be an office off the long hallway and shuts the door.

I should be relieved. Braxton De Luca is a wreck waiting to happen. He thinks I don't know that he can't possibly be good for me, but I do. I know. I see the darkness swirling around him. I see the cold, calculating man behind his eyes. I caught a glimpse of something sinister lurking in the shadows when he fucked me rough last night. Every inch of my body has told me to run in the opposite direction and run far whenever he's in the same room. The hairs on the back of my neck stand up, signaling danger. But instead of running, I want to get closer. The monster lurking beneath the surface has my curiosity piqued. I don't know what that says about me. I should be relieved that he let me go, then why am I disappointed?

Because despite my lack of experience with relationships or anything sexual, I want Braxton. I want him to mark me, to own me, to make me his in whichever way he deems fit. But this... this running away every time his conscience tells him he's no good for me isn't going to fly. And I'm calling bullshit.

"Miss."

My eyes snap to the guy wearing a black three-piece suit standing at the door to the garage and waiting patiently for me to gather my things. I hold up my hand in a 'give me a sec' gesture and make my way to the room Braxton disappeared into.

Not bothering to knock, I try the handle surprised that it isn't locked, and push my way through the door.

"You can't just walk–"

I swallow the rest of my words when four sets of eyes turn my way. Followed by three sets of smirks. Braxton's lips pull into a thin line, his jaw ticking and I know, I just know, that I'm in so much trouble. "I, uh, didn't know you had company. I'm sorry. I'll just…" I start backing toward the door.

"No need. We were just finishing up," the guy at the far end says, standing up, and I have to crane my neck because, damn he's tall. And built. Thick corded muscle barely encased in the black shirt he's wearing, a leather jacket hanging from his hand. Long jean covered legs and combat boots on his feet. Grey eyes stare back at me and his smirk grows into a grin when he realizes I'm staring. I swallow hard recognition dawning that he's the guy who barged into the office that night at the club.

A throat clears, and heat travels up my cheeks when I realize that Braxton just caught me staring at his friend, but Hulk doesn't waver in his own perusal of me.

"Alessandro." Braxton's voice is thick with warning.

Hulk chuckles, walking toward me, a shit eating grin plastered on his face. He stops next to me, his body within inches of mine. One thick finger trails down the side of my face, down my neck. A growl sounds from my left but Hulk doesn't remove his finger. Instead he leans down, his breath warm against my cheek. "Give him hell, baby girl." I shiver at the deepness of his voice.

"Swear to Christ, Alessandro. I'll remove that hand if you don't remove it from her."

Another man, this one just as tall, but not as built as Hulk steps forward, clapping him on the shoulder. His blue eyes twinkling in amusement as he looks from me to Hulk and then over to Braxton. His inky black hair shining in the bright sunlight streaming through the floor to ceiling window. "C'mon, Alex. Leave the poor girl alone." He tips his head. "Antonio," he says, proffering his hand for me to shake.

"Klara." I slip mine in his, but instead of a shake he grips my hand, turning it over and pulling it to his mouth to place a soft kiss close to my knuckles.

"Enough," Braxton barks, pushing up from his seat behind the large desk, making his way to my side and throwing an arm around my shoulders, pulling me back from Alessandro and Antonio. "You fuckers need to get out before I kill you."

The two men chuckle, moving out of Braxton's reach and away from me. "Awh, c'mon, Boss. Just having some fun."

Braxton glares at them mumbling something about no respect then tips his chin toward the third man who hasn't moved from his seat in one of the chairs facing the desk. "The only fucker I wouldn't have to kill is Giovanni. At least someone in this room still has respect."

Giovanni.

His eyes move from Braxton to me and I stop breathing. Cold, dead eyes glare at me from under thick dark lashes. Everything about him screams for me to not get close, to take cover behind Braxton or Antonio, or hell, even Alessandro. I wonder if Braxton sees it, too. Then he blinks and it's gone. Replaced by idle amusement at the scene in front of him and my reaction to him.

"Ciao." He pushes up from the chair, walking around us. Only stopping once he's halfway through the door and looks over his shoulder. "Let's go get this over with."

Antonio and Alessandro nod, following him out and I feel like I can breathe a little easier. That is until Braxton spins me into him, backing me up until the backs of my knees hit the desk.

"Did you like their hands on you, Mia Bella? Did you like Alessandro's touch or the way his breath skated across your skin?"

A hand wraps around my loose hair, tugging my head back and forcing my face up to his. "Did you like Antonio's mouth on you?"

His hand runs down my side, inching up the men's dress shirt I still have on, gripping my hip and pushing his into mine. His rigid length brushing against my belly. I moan.

"Do you want them, Mia Bella?" His teeth sink into my jaw, his tongue running along the same spot trying to sooth the sting. "Do you want their touch?"

"N-No. I want your touch, Brax. Only yours," I pant.

"Good answer." His grips my throat, fingers digging into my cheeks. "Now, I'm going to show you what happens when you interrupt a meeting." He lets go, stepping back and unbuckling his belt. "Get on your knees, Mia Bella."

I do as I'm as told, watching as Braxton undoes his zipper and slides his dress pants down to his ankles, followed by his boxer-briefs. He palms his thick dick, slowly stroking up and down the long length. "Going to fuck that sweet mouth, Mia Bella."

He reaches down, his thumb running across my bottom lip. "Been dreaming of these lips wrapped around my cock." He grips my chin in one hand, the other running the head of his cock across my lips making me open for him.

I've never sucked anyone off before. Not from lack of begging from previous boyfriends but I just never felt the desire to. Truth be told, until meeting Braxton I never wanted to. I was firmly in the 'I'd rather receive than give' group. Call me selfish but it was what it was. But now, after meeting Braxton, I want to do whatever it takes to please him. I want to make him happy, to see him come undone because of me.

I lick up his length, flicking the tip of my tongue up the slit before wrapping my lips around the head of his cock and taking him in my mouth. Braxton grunts when my nose hits his pelvis, the entire length of his cock buried down my throat. Courtesy of having my tonsils removed when I was little.

His hands grip the back of my head, fingers tangled in my long hair as he fucks my mouth without abandon. My little choking sounds stirring him on, making his hips thrusts harder. Moments later, I feel him swell against my tongue.

"Breathe through your nose, Mia Bella, and swallow every last drop," he grunts, moments before he explodes down my throat. I'm surprised by the taste, it's nothing like I expected, and I'm looking forward to doing it again.

Braxton tucks himself back in his pants, his fingers gripping my chin and pulling me up until I'm standing in front of him. His hands brush my hair away from my face, his fingers curling around my nape. He rests his forehead on mine, our eyes so close gazing into each other. "Don't ever interrupt another meeting again, yeah?"

I swallow and nod, my core clenching from the demand in his voice. "I'm sorry. I didn't know you were in a meeting. You just walked away from me," I whine, then instantly cringe at the sound of my voice. I don't whine. Ever.

"Klara," he growls, turning his back on me, running a hand through his hair.

"Look, I get that you think you're no good for me. That you're this big bad wolf and you have to protect me from yourself, but I'm a big girl, Braxton. I can protect myself. Been doing it all my life. Let me in, Brax," I plead.

He turns on me, backing me into the desk until my back is bent over it. His hand running down my throat to my collarbone. "Can you? Protect yourself?" His eyes roam over all the bruises decorating my throat down to the ones on my hips. "You couldn't protect yourself from my touch, Klara. If I let you in. If I let you stay, it'll be more than just bruises decorating your pretty skin. Couldn't live with myself if something happened to you because of me."

"You won't hurt me," I whisper, my eyes growing hooded against his fingers on my body. As soon as the words leave my mouth, the heat from his body is gone. Braxton retreats to the other side of the room, far away from me.

"It's not me I'm worried about." He turns to look out over the city.

The view from up here is out of this world. I could spend hours sitting by one of the many floor to ceiling windows on this side of the house and just stare out over Toronto, and the harbor in the distance. I've always been an ocean girl. Always been drawn to the water, always wanted to wake up to the sound of rolling waves. But this, this view of Braxton in a tailored suit standing by the huge window and looking out over the city. I would trade the ocean for more views like this.

"What do you dream of at night, Klara? A husband? Kids? A house with a picket fence?" His voice is deep, gravelly when he finally speaks.

I shrug despite the fact that his back is to me. "Eventually. Yeah, I guess."

Braxton doesn't respond, he just nods continuing his stare out the window, his hands resting casually in the pockets of his dress pants. He looks relaxed. Like a young CEO who has the world at his fingertips. Except I know that's not true. I can see the slight stiffness in his shoulders, the way his back is ramrod straight. The man in front of me is the furthest thing from relaxed at this moment.

"Won't ever be able to give you that dream, Klara. No picket fence. No kids." He looks over his shoulder at me. "No husband."

My stomach sinks. How did this conversation get so personal so fast? We haven't known each other long, and now he's talking marriage and kids. But I realize that's not why my stomach sinks and I feel like I'm going to be sick. No, it's because deep down I want it. All of it. The house. The kids. And I want it with him.

Fuck me.

It only took a handful of days for Braxton De Luca to get under my skin to the point where I was dreaming about a life with him. Dreaming about waking up next to him every morning, falling asleep against him every night. Heck, wasn't I just thinking about giving up my dream of living by the ocean so that I could see Braxton every day. And now he's telling me I have no chance of ever having any of it.

Well, fuck him.

"You're giving me whiplash, Braxton. You're hot one minute. Cold the next. If you don't want me, then why invite me to spend the week here with you?"

Finally, he turns around to face me. But I see the minute it happens. All his walls close down and the man in front of me isn't the Braxton I've been coming to know.

"Needed a warm body in my bed, babe." He winks, walking over to the makeshift bar in the office and pouring himself a couple fingers of the amber liquid.

I feel like I've just been punched in the gut but I refuse to let him see what his words do to me. Instead I steel my shoulders, lift my chin and pray to God my eyes don't give me away.

"You're an asshole, De Luca. But lucky for you, I was just looking for a good fuck." I let my eyes roam down his body one last time before meeting his hard gaze again. "Well, good is being generous. I'll go gather my things."

Fuck, Klara, don't cry. Don't you dare fucking cry for that asshole.

Don't cry. Don't cry.

I repeat the mantra to myself as I go about gathering my torn dress and panties from Braxton's room. Cold realization that I never had a chance to go back to my apartment to get clothes before coming back here sinks in. Rummaging through a dresser, I pull out a pair of Braxton's sweatpants and pull them on, tying them on the side so that they don't fall down. I'll have to find his driver again and get him to drive me back to my place, because there's no way I'm taking the bus looking like this, or a cab for that matter. I look like shit. Worse than shit actually.

The bedroom door flies open, bouncing off the wall with a bang. Braxton is standing on the other side, seething, his hands clenching and unclenching into fists, his knuckles turning white.

Oh, fuck.

"Good, Klara?"

I swallow hard, backing up when he stalks toward me, his nostril flaring. Braxton cages me in, my back pressed up against the wall, his hands on either side of my head. His face so close to mine, all I have to do is lean forward half an inch.

"Good was being generous?" He repeats my words back to me.

My throat goes dry. I never could keep a leash on my tongue when my anger got the best of me, and now I was paying for it.

"Klara."

My eyes follow the bob of his Adam's apple, up his strong jaw until they connect with his. I never thought it was possible but his dark eyes are even darker, almost a black hole sucking me in. My tongue licks across my bottom lip, pulling it between my teeth, and I watch as his eyes get impossibly darker.

"I can't control myself around you, Klara." He buries his nose in the curve of my neck. "I can't let you go no matter how much I try." His teeth graze my ear and I shiver, curling my fingers into his hips, pulling him closer. "But you need to tell me when I hurt you."

When, not if. I give myself a mental shake, not wanting to go there now. Not when he's so close. We both have issues that we have to work through before this can become anything more. But those issues will still be there in the light of day tomorrow. Right now, for the rest of today, I want to lose myself in Braxton. I want to surrender everything to him.

"Okay," I whisper, my lips brushing against his ear.

Braxton stills, his face never leaving the curve of my neck. His lips pressing against the pulse point in my neck. "Kitten."

"What?" I tilt my face, allowing him more access.

"Your safe word. If you need me to stop. If it gets too much. Use it." His breath tickles my skin, sending another shiver down my body.

My eyes close and I nod.

Braxton growls. "Klara, need to hear you say that you'll use it if you need it. Say the words, baby."

"Okay," I breathe.

Braxton's fingers trail down my arms, grip my wrists and bring them up, pinning them above my head in his iron grip. His other hand roaming down the side of my face to wrap around my throat. Strong fingers digging into my cheeks forcing me to look up at him.

"What's your safe word, Klara?"

"K-Kitten," I gulp.

"Good girl." His lips descend on mine in a bruising kiss, his hand never leaving my throat. "Keep your hands up here," he whispers near my ear and I nod.

His fingers curl around the fabric of the dress shirt I'm still wearing and he rips it, buttons flying in every direction. Pressing open mouth kisses along my collarbone and between my breasts, Braxton curls his fingers in the waistband of the sweatpants next, pushing them down my legs as he kneels in front of me, continuing his lazy kisses down my stomach and just below my belly button.

Except for the shirt hanging open at my sides now, I'm completely naked and vulnerable in front of a still very much dressed Braxton. Placing a hand on each of my thighs, he nudges them apart until I readjust my stance.

"Do not come, Klara," he rasps.

"Wha--? Ah."

My head falls back against the wall when his tongue licks up my slit, swirling around my clit before closing his lips around it and sucking. My knees try to buckle but Braxton grips my hips, holding me up and against the wall.

His tongue runs up my slit again, flicking my clit once. Twice. Before licking up my slit again. Each time the tip of his tongue dips between my folds a little before retreating and continuing his torture. My hips buck beneath his mouth. I need to touch him, to keep his mouth where I want it. Where I need it. I can feel myself climbing higher. Then his mouth is gone and I groan.

"I mean it, Klara. Do not come. I'll punish you if you let this pussy come around anything other than my cock."

Punish me? Wait, hold up.

I want to tell him that I didn't sign up for any punishment, but then his mouth is back on me, sucking my clit between those full lips, and I forget why I ever wanted him to stop.

"Ah, fuck. Braxton, please…"

He thrusts two fingers inside me, his tongue continuing its rhythm on my clit. "Please what?" He blows against my clit and I shudder.

"Please make me come," I groan, bucking and grinding my hips onto his hand.

His slips his hand from my pussy, onyx eyes looking up at me. Braxton smirks, standing up he runs his fingers, still wet from being buried in my pussy, along my lips before forcing his fingers into my mouth. "Suck," he commands, and I obey, watching as his eyes grow hooded and his nose flares.

"Enough." He removes his fingers from my mouth, grips the back of my head in his hand, my throat in the other, then he's kissing me, and it's nothing like I've ever experienced. It's carnal. Hungry.

Owning. His teeth sink into my bottom lip making me whimper. "Get on the bed. On your knees. Ass up."

Again, I do as I'm told. Moving to the middle of the bed, I shed the dress shirt and bend over at the waist. Offering up my ass to him. Warm fingers run up my back, wrapping my long hair around a fist and tugging until I'm forced to arch my back.

"Now's the time to use that safe word, Klara, because once I have you again I'll never be able to walk away from you. You'll be mine," he growls close to my ear, and I realize he's naked. At least his top half is. "And good will be the last fucking thing on your mind when you think about my cock inside you."

"Please, Braxton," I beg when his fingers push inside me again.

"That's not your safe word, baby."

I try shaking my head but the grip he has around my hair isn't allowing any movement. "I-I don't." I swallow hard and try again. "Please, fuck me."

He growls, removing his fingers, and just when I think he may actually give me what I want—

Smack!

I yelp when his palm connects with the flesh of my ass, and then moan when he gently smooths his hand over the stinging area.

"Try again, Klara. This time, I want you to call me sir." His fingers thrust in again, his thumb finding and circling my nub.

"Ah, fuck me," I groan, feeling my climax growing closer.

Smack!

Braxton's palm hits my other ass cheek and I yelp again not expecting the spank a second, third, fourth time.

"Please, fuck me, Sir," I moan.

The hand not wrapped around my hair grips my chin, tilting my face back forcing me to look over my shoulder at him as he licks up my neck.

"Don't come until I tell you to."

His nips at my jaw. Little mewls escape my throat when I feel his cock slide between my ass cheeks. Then in one fluid motion, he thrusts into me and I cry out at the sudden intrusion. Not because it hurts. It feels fucking amazing. But because I'm trying like hell to not come.

"So tight," he growls. "So fucking perfect."

Braxton pulls me up, anchoring my arms behind my back in one of his. His other hand wrapping around my throat, causing my head to fall back against his shoulder. Then he really starts fucking me. His hips pivoting, his cock pounding in and out. In and out.

"Ah, shit! Ah, fuck!"

The head of his cock hitting my g-spot on every upward thrust has me almost coming undone. I need to come, and I need to come hard. His fingers leave my throat to trail down my middle until they're reaching between my legs. I try to move, but it's impossible.

His long fingers find my clit and it's too much. There's no way I can hold on any longer.

"Please, Sir. Please let me come."

Braxton chuckles, like he's enjoying watching me squirm. He removes his fingers from my clit, his thrusts stop and he let's go of my arm causing me to fall forward on the bed. Breathing hard, I want to cry out in frustration.

He flips me over onto my back, pushing his way between my legs, guiding the head of his cock into my pussy. "Wrap your legs around my waist, Klara."

I do. Braxton sits back on his knees, his fingers curling into my hips. His thrusts getting harder. Faster.

"Come for me, Mia Bella. Come around my cock."

The sound of the pet name leaving his lips, the feel of his cock hitting my g-spot, his fingers rubbing circles around my clit. It's all too much. I'm in sensory overload, but my body accepts his command, and I come so fucking hard, arching my back, gripping the bed sheets in my fists, his name on my lips.

I'm so lost in my own orgasmic bliss that I feel more than hear Braxton find his own release. The distant thought that we never used protection this time floating through my mind but I'm too sated, too tired to do anything about it right now.

My lids droop closed right as I feel the bed dip. Make-up sex is my new favorite thing.

NINE

IT'S BEEN TWO weeks since that night and I've only left Braxton's house to grab clean clothes from my apartment, and to start my new summer job at the local gym as a Zumba instructor. Things have started changing in the last two weeks.

I no longer wake up in fear that Braxton won't be lying beside me, or that he'll change his mind about us again. Gio and I have also started a weird sort of friendship as well.

It all started a week into my staying at Braxton's. I was in a bitchy mood and probably PMS'ing; slamming doors in the kitchen. So much so that one minute I was alone, and the next I had the four amigos staring at me in mild curiosity from Braxton's office door. I may have flipped them off before stomping off to our bedroom.

And okay, when did I start thinking about it as our bedroom?

Braxton hadn't touched me in three days. And I get it, I wouldn't want him touching me below the waist during that time of month either. But he didn't touch me at all. No cuddling, no little sensual touches, no make-out sessions. The only thing I got were little pecks on my cheek. So yeah, I was frustrated and bitchy as shit.

The next day when I padded to the kitchen for my morning coffee, Gio was already there. When I quirked an eyebrow in question as to why he was here so much earlier than the others, he just grinned, dropped a plastic grocery bag on the counter, and pulled out a pint of Ben & Jerry's Half-Baked ice cream. I may have almost torn his hand off in my haste to grab the pint and open it as fast as my fingers would allow. He chuckled, then proceeded to pull out my favourite milk chocolate bar, caramel filled chocolates, and when I thought he was done... then continued to pull out a white to-go coffee cup with a green logo from behind his back. Is it weird to develop a crush on one of your boyfriend's best friends because he brings you chocolate, ice cream, and coffee when your PMS'ing? Asking for a friend.

Gio and I spent the rest of that day and the rest of the week binge watching episodes of The Vampire Diaries. We never discussed anything outside of the show. I didn't ask about his life and he didn't ask about mine, or my relationship with his friend. It was like somehow, he knew that the only thing I needed that week was to veg out on the couch with chocolate and Netflix, but that I didn't want to be alone, and Braxton was in and out of meetings constantly the last two weeks, and that, coupled with his lack of affection, was starting to grate on my nerves.

"Is it always going to be like this?" I ask Gio between episodes.

He shrugs, taking a drink of his coffee. "It's his job, Klara. This life," he pauses, not looking away from the TV. "This life isn't easy."

"I think I've seen you more the last two weeks than I have him."

"He's an important man, Klara."

When I glance at Gio, his lips are pulled in a thin line, his hands curled in fists on his lap. I want to ask him if he wasn't supposed to tell me that, after all, Braxton hasn't even told me what he does for a living. Finance is all I get out of him when I ask about his job. It's all I've ever gotten.

"What does he do, Gio?"

I know it's a wasted effort, but I at least have to try and weasel information out of Gio.

"It's best you don't know," is all he says while checking his phone.

His answer did nothing to appease my curiosity. I've never been a nosy person. Okay, that's a lie. I've always been a nosy person. Usually trying to get the inside scoop on people's lives by eavesdropping. It's a habit I've been trying to break since I was a kid. My mom always says that when I was a baby, if I ever heard voices in the room while I was sleeping, I would instantly be awake and looking around for the owners of said voices. It only got worse the older I got.

But is it wrong for me to want to know everything about my boyfriend? Well, all the important stuff anyway. Like maybe what he does for a living? I don't think so. And all this secrecy is only serving to up my frustration.

Gio eyes me, mischief dancing behind his hazel eyes.

"What?" I ask, chuckling when he doesn't look away.

He doesn't immediately respond, instead switches off the TV, gathering up his wallet. Only when he's halfway to the interior garage door does he pause and turn to look over at me, inclining his head. "Let's go. Been cooped up here long enough."

"Where are we going?" I ask, snatching up my purse from a stool at the breakfast bar and following him out to the garage and over to the blacked-out SUV.

"You'll see." He smirks.

Pulling my lip between my teeth, I glance toward the door to the house wondering why one of his best friends is making the effort to spend time with me while he couldn't be less interested. Then I decide to stop thinking. Braxton has been in non-stop meetings, barely acknowledging my presence, so what if I was tired of hanging around his house all day by myself. I needed fresh air, and I trust Gio.

Close to thirty minutes later, Gio miraculously manages to find a parking spot right outside of the CN Tower. I still have no idea what we're doing, but I follow him inside the tall building. Only once he's paid for our ticket and we're stepping off the elevator does he turn his megawatt smile on me.

"Ever done the EdgeWalk?"

"Have I ever done the walk around the outside of the tower with only a harness to protect me?" I ask, eyebrow raised in a 'what do you think' way and crossing my arms under my chest.

He grins. "Yeah."

I shake my head, hoping he's not suggesting what I think he is. "That would be a no, Gio."

His grin grows and my stomach falls.

No.

I drop my arms, backing away. "No. Nope. No way. Not going to happen."

"Come on, Klara. Live a little. I won't let anything happen to you. Promise."

"Gio, me and heights don't have a great relationship." I shrug, looking over at the diminishing line of people waiting for their turn at the EdgeWalk.

Gio smirks, raising an eyebrow as he glances behind him at the line and slowly starts backing away from me, arms raised in surrender. "Alright, I get it. I'll come find you when I'm done," he says, then turns around and proceeds to get in line behind the last couple of people.

I take in the growing crowd around me and curse. The bastard knows I hate large crowds from our numerous talks over the last couple weeks. So, it's no coincidence that he didn't put up a bigger fight to get me to go with him. Asshole knew that I'll have to decide between staying inside while the crowd slowly grows around me from tourists, or join him on the walk where our group is limited to six.

I sigh, and make my way toward Gio, where he's getting into an orangey-red jumpsuit.

"Okay. Okay. I'm coming."

***

"How are you doing?" Gio asks from behind me, and I have to fight the reaction to glance back at him. Because looking back would mean that I would have even more of an urge to look down. We're over one thousand feet up right now, and looking down is not high on my list of things to do at this moment.

91

And then, like our guide can sense my unease, he instructs us one by one to step forward and put our toes by the edge and look down.

I'm sorry, look down? Is he mad?

Because Gio is last in line, he gets to go first, and I swear the man has no fear because he just does it with no reservation, and he lets go of the rope tethering us to the line above us. Fuck that shit. When Gio steps back to the middle of the landing, it's my turn. My toes don't come close to the edge because fuck, that's a long way down, and even though the rope attached to us is said to be able to hold about three-hundred pounds, I still don't quite trust it.

I breathe a little easier when I step back to the middle, and the others in front of me have their turn. But then I watch in horror when our guide has us turn around and slowly back toward the edge and lean over it!

Yup, lean over it! Is everyone in this city crazy?

Our guide must given up on me when I barely lean back because for the rest of the twenty or thirty minutes we're up here, he doesn't call on me to try his crazy stunt moves. Gio laughs behind me, and I've never wanted to punch someone's balls as much as I just want to sock him one.

Fifteen minutes into the walk and I'm slowly starting to relax. I still refuse to look down or lean over the edge but I have to admit that the skyline from up here is beautiful. My body jerks slightly to the right— toward the edge—and panic starts setting in, then Gio's hands wrap around my waist bringing me closer to the building and holding me steady.

"You okay?"

It's windy enough up here that if he wasn't so close I wouldn't've been able to hear him. I nod trying to swallow past my suddenly dry throat and trying to trample down the panic that arose. Gio stays close behind me for the rest of the walk, and I'm slightly thankful, and slightly fearful.

I know I didn't slip, and I definitely didn't trip over my own feet. No, it almost felt like I was pushed. I mentally give myself a shake and shut that thought down. There's no way Gio would've pushed me. We're strapped into a harness that's hooked to a steel line above us. He should know that I'm not going anywhere unless he magically got my harness unhooked. And Braxton would kill him. But he did manage to catch me fast, which means he must have been right behind me when I tripped.

For heaven's sake, Klara. Being so high up is screwing with your head. Gio did not just try to push you over the edge.

I want to collapse in a relieved pile on the floor when we re-enter the building and start unhooking the rope and getting out of our harnesses.

TEN

BRAXTON IS FUMING when we arrive back at the house and calls Gio into his office. Alessandro walks by Gio, clasping a hand on his shoulder and shakes his head.

Well, that can't be good.

"Have a good time, baby girl?" Alessandro grabs an apple from the fruit bowl on the breakfast bar and tosses it up in the air before effortlessly catching it in one hand.

I shrug. "It was fun, I guess. Not a fan of heights, but it was okay."

He nods, eyeing me as he bites into the green fruit. "Didn't think to let us know where ya were going?" he asks behind a mouth full.

I twist off the cap to my water and level him with a glare. "It was last minute. Plus, I didn't think Braxton would mind. You know, seeing as how he's been doing nothing but taking meetings all day every day since I've been here."

Alessandro doesn't respond while he finishes the apple and tosses the core in the garbage. "He'll always want to know where you are, baby girl. Your safety is important to him."

"My safety?" I cross my arms under my chest and lean a hip into the counter. "I was with Gio. I think I was plenty safe, Alex." My eyes narrow, noticing the fact that Alessandro refuses to make eye contact with me and keeps running a hand over his bald head. "What exactly does he do, Alex? What exactly do all of you do? And don't give me that finance bullshit."

His lips twitch like he's trying not to smile at my outburst then he curses. That damn hand running over his head again. Finally, he drags his grey eyes up to my face his mouth opening and closing like he's trying to find the right words to say.

"Klara. My office," Braxton bellows from behind me and I jump.

Alessandro smirks, picking up another apple from the bowl. "Give him hell, baby girl," he says before turning and exiting through the garage door.

When I walk into his office, Gio is nowhere to be found. I frown in confusion, certain that I hadn't seen him slip out while Alessandro and I were talking in the kitchen. Braxton lowers himself into the massive black leather office chair behind his desk, steepling his fingers in front of him and leaning his elbows on the desk. His dark eyes boring into mine.

Lord, give me the strength to deal with this man. I silently pray as I take the chair across from him and automatically shift in my seat under his watchful gaze.

"Should've told me where you were going, Klara. Don't like not knowing where you are."

I sit up straighter, pulling my shoulders back, and force myself to look him in the eyes. "Am I your hostage, Braxton?"

That seems to take him by surprise. His eyebrows shoot up to his hairline, his posture going stiff, then he quickly corrects it. The laid-back CEO-type reemerging. "What kind of question is that, Mia Bella?"

"Am I being held here against my will, Braxton?" I repeat my previous question.

He leans back in his chair, crossing an ankle over a knee. His long fingers playing with a pen on his desk. "You know you're not."

I nod, still refusing to let my eyes wonder away from his face. "Then, if I'm free to go as I please I see nothing wrong with what I did. I was feeling cooped up in your house. Ignored while you took meeting after meeting, and Gio sensed it. He got me out of the house for a couple hours and I'm thankful for it. Something my boyfriend should be wanting to do not one of his friends."

He props his other elbow on the armrest of the chair, running a thumb over his bottom lip making my thighs squeeze together.

"Look, Braxton." I sigh, looking out the huge window and over the city. "If you're going to be in meetings all day while I'm here and only spending time with me to get laid, then I'd rather not come over anymore. I'm not some sex object you can use whenever the mood strikes and then forget about when something more important comes along. I don't even know what you do for a living, Brax."

"It's my job, Klara. It doesn't take a break, and neither can I."

I deflate a little at his statement, not missing that he still didn't answer my question about what his job is. I nod, refusing to move my gaze from the scenery out the window.

96

Am I wrong to be hung up on something like not knowing what his job is? I don't think I am. I think that him refusing to answer my question actually says a lot. It's fucking job. It shouldn't be this hard for him to tell me what he does. And if he can so easily hide it then what else is he hiding. I refuse to keep pursuing a relationship with someone who doesn't show even a sliver of guilt for hiding something from me, and I'm so fucking tired of this back and forth shit. A relationship is about give and take, and so far it's been Braxton taking and demanding with no give.

"I'll get out of your way then," I say in a voice that sounds a little too defeated, and force myself to stand from the chair.

"It's late. Stay the night. I'll get Pete to drive you back in the morning."

***

I probably should've just left, but I couldn't bring myself to pack my bag and sneak out while he was working. So here I am. Propped up against the headboard of our bed, in the only pajamas I brought, with a book that I'm not paying attention to. I think I've read the same few lines over and over again. My eyes take in the words, but my brain is on the other side of the house in Braxton's office.

"What time is your class at the gym tomorrow?" Braxton asks, undoing his tie as he walks into our bedroom.

Dammit, I have to stop thinking of it as our bedroom. It's his house. His bedroom.

"Not 'til late. Why?"

He unbuttons the first few buttons of his dress shirt, sitting on the bed next to me while I bookmark the page I'm reading.

"I want you to meet me for lunch tomorrow." The light from the bedside table is just bright enough to bask him in a soft glow. He looks almost angelic like this. The top few buttons of his shirt undone, his sleeves rolled up revealing toned forearms, his usual slicked back hair looking disheveled from the countless times he's run a hand through the dark locks. But Braxton is anything but angelic. "At my office," he adds when I don't respond to his invitation.

My mouth drops open, throat dry, sure that I misheard him.

"I thought you were going to be in meetings all day tomorrow, too?"

He leans his elbows on his knees, looking slightly over his shoulder at me. His eyes roam down the top half of my body not covered by the sheet. Absentmindedly my tongue runs over my bottom lip and I watch as Braxton eyes it. Heat blazing to life behind his gaze. He reaches for my book, placing it on the bedside table before crawling up my body, leaning his elbows on either side of my head.

"I will be. That's exactly why you need to have lunch with me. Make me look forward to something while I'm sitting through boring meetings."

"Braxton." I run my palms down his chest, savoring the feel of hard skin beneath them. "I don't want to distract you. I'll just go home, and you can call me when you feel like opening up to me."

"You were right, Mia Bella." He nuzzles the crook of my neck, kissing just under my ear. "It wasn't fair of me to bring you here with the intention of spending time with you, only to ignore you. I'm sorry."

His fingers start roaming my body and I'm lost in all things De Luca when his lips rejoin the action. Braxton pushes my panties to the side, unzips his pants, and my legs wrap around his waist as he pushes into me.

We're still fully clothed, but I don't care, because I'm where I need to be. In his arms.

ELEVEN

"**T**HIS IS YOUR office?" I ask, my jaw hitting the floor as I take in the spacious room.

Floor to ceiling windows take up the entire right side and the far wall lending to an incredible view of the city. A large mahogany desk on the far side. A wet bar decorates the left side next to a door which I'm assuming is either a bathroom or a really huge closet.

Braxton chuckles, leaning against his closed office door, hands casually stuffed into the pockets of his dress pants and an easy smile pulling at his lips. "It is."

I feel like such an idiot pushing him to tell me the truth about what he does when he has been truthful this whole time. He does actually work in finance. Investing specifically. The building his office is housed in is the tallest on the block. Luca Enterprises spanning the top of the building.

Braxton had met me down in the lobby when it was time for our lunch date, filling me in that he had already made reservations and we were about to be late.

Reservations turned out to be at a cute little Greek restaurant not too far from his building. He laughed when I confessed that Greek food was my favourite, and if I had to pick one food to eat for the rest of my life, it would probably be that. He sat grinning at me when I divulged that my love of the culture's food fed into my desire to one day to travel to Greece and explore all the islands. Starting with Santorini, because hello, Sisterhood of the Traveling Pants. He mostly choked on his water when I told him that it was my favorite movie and for the sole purpose that part of it was set on the Greek island.

I found out that Greek food is also his favorite, and that he has already been to Greece, but loved it so much he wouldn't mind going back one day. And no, his love of the islands did not stem from his love of the food, and he has not seen that particular movie yet, which I plan to rectify soon.

His love of the islands actually stemmed from the insane amount of traveling he did as a child. Whenever his dad was bogged down with endless meetings and phone calls, his mom would pack him and his sister up and the three of the them would travel somewhere new together for a couple weeks before returning home. I guess workaholics ran in their family.

It worries me that Braxton may be following in his father's footsteps. His dad died at age fifty from a sudden heart attack. The man worked twelve-hour days, seven days a week. Never took a vacation in his life, except for when he got married, and the day Braxton was born. If this thing between us continues to grow then I'm not okay with waking up one morning to realize that Braxton died from a heart attack, just like his father because he was overworked. No amount of work is as important as his life.

After lunch, we grab a couple coffees and drink them as we walk aimlessly around the downtown streets. He tells me more about his parents and his upbringing, although, I get the feeling that he is holding back a lot from me, too. And I tell him more about my family, and about Adrienne and our friendship. I was pretty much on my own since both my parents died in a car accident just after I graduated high school. They were on one of their weekly date nights when a drunk driver on their phone drove through a red light and hit them at full speed. The only relief was that they died on impact. Well, I don't look at it as a relief, but that's what the doctor at the hospital had said, and I guess it was better than them being in pain, but there was no relief to losing both my parents on the same night.

Soon after that I moved in with Adrienne. She helped me dig my way out of the dark hell I found myself in after their deaths, and the rest, they say, is history. Other than a couple years I did in an exchange program that sent me to Colorado, it's been Dri and I ever since the death of my parents. I wouldn't trade my friendship with Dri for anything. She's my rock, my best friend, and sometimes a pain in my ass, but I love her. Shortly after I met Adrienne, Rick came into the picture, and the three of us have been inseparable. The three musketeers.

Braxton told me more about what he does for a living. He's a private lender of sorts, and he helps people invest their money where they could get a better return than if they went to a bank. Numbers aren't my thing, so I just smiled and nodded whenever he would go into depth explaining about investments and returns. Eventually he laughed, slipped his hand into mine, and changed the subject while we continued our walk back to his office.

When I asked about the guys, he just shrugged and said that he and Antonio grew up together. They were practically brothers. He met Alessandro—Alex—in high school. Alex was the new kid in school with the weird accent so Braxton took him in essentially, and they've been best friends ever since. I was surprised to know that he only met Gio in recent years but that they clicked when Braxton's cousin, Dante, introduced them at the club. Which I also found out was owned by Dante and not Braxton, but he still got all the perks because family was family and they took care of their own.

I wasn't ready to call it a day yet when we got back to the office building and neither was Braxton. Fast forward a few minutes, and that's how I ended up standing in the middle of his corner office with my jaw on the floor and staring out over the city.

"I can't get over this view."

Braxton grins, placing a finger under my chin and helping me close my mouth, then he wraps his arms around my middle and pulls me back into him. "It's one of the reasons I bought the building. The view on the first several floors is shit but once you clear the buildings…it's incredible. And it's the same thing all around. The other side of the building is the same unobstructed view."

"It must look amazing at night with all the lights of the city."

"Hmm," Braxton hums, his chest vibrating against my back as he licks up my neck. "You know what else would look amazing?"

I giggle, knowing exactly where he's going with this. "What's that?"

97

He nips at my ear. "You bent over my desk." He groans when I push my ass back into his crotch.

"Can anyone see us up here?"

Braxton's lips trail fiery kisses down my neck and I shudder. "We can see out, but no one can see in," he says, moving my hair over one shoulder to give himself better access as he continues kissing along my shoulder.

"Is the door locked?"

Shivers race down my body when I feel his lips quirk in a smile against my heated skin. "No, so you'll have to be extra quiet. Think you can manage that, Mia Bella?"

Turning in his arms, I hook one hand around his nape bringing his mouth down on mine while my other hand cups the hard bulge behind his zipper.

"Baby, it's you who has to be quiet," I whisper against his lips. "Think you can manage that?" I smirk as I fight to undo his belt buckle and unzip his pants.

"Boss, we got a problem." His office door flies open and I want to curse the day he ever met the two men standing in the door way.

Braxton blows out a hard breath, redoing his pants before turning toward the imposing figures. "That's the second fucking time, Alessandro," he growls.

I want to rip a strip into them too but then I catch a glimpse of Alessandro and Gio's hands. The same hands they're trying desperately to hide behind their backs or under crossed arms when they realize that Braxton is not alone.

"Is that blood? Why is there blood on your hands?"

Out of the corner of my eye I see Braxton turn to stone, his gaze taking in everything in front of him. I try to squint to get a better look because, yup, there's tiny splatters of blood on both their shirts as well.

What the hell?

Two sets of eyes, one grey and one dark, ping pong between me and Braxton before settling on him as if looking to him for answers.

"I'd hate to see the other fucker," Braxton says, his calm voice contradicting the stillness to his body.

Gio grins as Alessandro shrugs. "Fucker thought he had the jump on us. He wanted a fight, he got one."

"Fight? The two of you got into a fight?" I take several steps forward in my resolve to check them out, to make sure they're okay, but they both take a synchronized step back like they've practiced this dance many times before.

"It's nothing, baby girl. We're fine. Just some idiots wanting to prove something." Alessandro smiles reassuringly, but it's a lie. I've been around the two of them long enough over the last several weeks to tell when they're lying, or trying to protect me from the truth.

I'm not some fragile thing though, dammit. I don't need protecting from the truth. I whirl on Braxton, ready to tell them as much, but am stunned he's standing right behind me catching me off guard.

"Pete is downstairs waiting to take you back to your apartment. I'll see you after your class, Mia Bella." His strong arms pull me into me as he places a soft kiss to my forehead and I melt a little inside. All the fight leaves me when I'm surrounded by Braxton.

TWELVE

One Week later

STEPPING OFF THE elevator on my floor, I dig around the bottom of my purse for my keys and stop short when black dress shoes appear in my line of sight. My lips automatically tipping in a smile because I know those dress shoes. They're the same ones that have met me here after each of my classes the last week.

Braxton.

"Hey, babe." I reach up on my tiptoes to place a kiss on his lips, and then unlock the door, stepping aside to let him in.

He takes off his suit jacket and tie as soon as he enters the quiet apartment, dropping them on the back of the couch and unbuttoning the top buttons of his dress shirt as he makes his way to the kitchen.

This is a new side of him I haven't seen before. I'm not used to this quiet, pensive version standing in front of me pouring us two glasses of my favorite wine.

Braxton replaces the wine in the fridge, his eyes downcast when he turns around, and without a word downs his entire glass of the sweet white wine.

"Brax?"

I gasp when he finally looks up, the weight of his dark gaze trained on me when he rounds the counter separating us and pulls me into him. One hand pressed into my lower back anchoring me to him while his other snakes under my hair, gripping my nape, his lips descending onto mine.

This kiss is nothing like we've shared before. It's not primal, it's not hungry, it's not owning. It's sweet, lazy, explorative. A sob escapes me at the realization of what this might mean, but Braxton doesn't let me go when I try leaning away and breaking the kiss. The hand on my lower back presses me closer, the hand around my nape holding me in place while he kisses me, and I feel it down to my very soul.

He kisses down my jaw while I continue to sob, my hands fisting his shirt in a silent plea. He picks me up, my legs wrapping around his waist, and carries me back into my room. Closing and locking the door behind us, all the while continuing to place openmouthed kisses down my neck and along my collarbone.

Braxton takes his time undressing me. Kissing each inch of skin as the fabric of my clothes pass over it. I return the favor when he has me completely naked. His body is a like a work of art sculpted from the finest clay.

His eyes squeeze shut and he swallows hard when my lips wrap around the head of his cock sucking him down my throat.

"Shit," he hisses when his cock hits the back of my throat over and over again. If this is supposed to be goodbye, then I'm going to make sure he doesn't forget a second of it.

Braxton pulls me up, throwing me down on the bed. I slide further up the bed until his hands wrap around my ankles stop my retreat. His head dips between my legs, that tongue I love so much bringing me to the edge, but not allowing me to tumble over.

When he crawls up the rest of my body, I see the pain he's trying to mask behind his eyes. The regret.

"Brax, you okay?" I ask, framing his face in my hands. It's a stupid question. I know this, and yet it's the only one I can think of to ask in this moment.

He dips his chin in a slight nod, placing a kiss on the tip of my nose. "Need to lose myself in you tonight, Mia Bella. Need to feel you surround me."

He kisses my forehead, my closed lids, my tear-stained cheeks. He continues to rain little kisses all over my body as he pushes into me. There are no spankings, no demands, no roughness tonight. Tonight, Braxton De Luca makes love to me like it'll be the last time. Tonight, his fingers and tongue trace over every dip, every curve of my skin like he's trying to memorize the way I look, the way I feel beneath him.

And when he finally brings me to the brink, it's by staring into his onyx eyes and wishing with all hope that this isn't how we end.

"Don't want this evil life to touch you, Mia Bella. Please forgive me," was all I heard as my eyes drooped closed and I drifted off to sleep.

***

I was surprised when I woke up this morning and he was still lying next to me, his fingers drawing lazy circles on my naked back. I fully expected him to be long gone by the time morning rolled around. What threw me for even more of a loop was when he told me to come by the office and have lunch with him today. Last night was almost too perfect. Almost too thought out by him, and my head already knows what my heart refuses to accept. That Braxton made love to me because it's his way of saying goodbye.

For good this time.

That theory was confirmed when I walk into his office for our lunch date. I push through the heavy door and stop dead in my tracks. My jaw drops in disbelief. I should turn around and run, I should scream, cry, ask him why he chose to end it this way instead of just leaving last night. But all I can think of... all that plays through my mind is me grabbing a hold of the bitch's hair and pounding her head into the glass desk she's currently bent over. I want to smash her face in until the only possible outcome is plastic surgery. I want to rip out her fake blonde extensions and feed them to her. I want to take a pair of metal pliers to her fake fingernails and rip them off one by one.

But like a deer in headlights, the only thing I do is stare at the scene unfolding in front of me. Well... the scene Braxton wants me to see. I'm not naïve, I know he set this all up so I would walk in at this exact moment and catch him in the act. So I would be the one to end it, because after all, he did promise me he wouldn't be the one to call a quits again.

What he hadn't been banking on, I'm guessing, is that I would see through it all. I would see the pain and regret in his eyes as he wraps his fist around her hair, just like he did mine, as he lowers his zipper and gets ready to enter her.

I won't give him the dignity of watching me crumble though. Taking a deep breath, I square my shoulders, lift my chin, and try valiantly to not let the tears fall. I lock eyes with the bitch bent over in front of him and smirk.

"Oh, honey, at least get yourself a real man." I'm surprised when my voice comes out sounding strong, even to my own ears, and then, when I feel like I have a lock on my emotions, I allow my stare to travel up to Braxton's to make sure my words hit their mark like I had hoped.

Braxton flinches. It's small but it is there. Taking one last strengthening breath, I turn and walk out of his office, holding my head up the entire way to the elevator, down to the parking garage and my car.

Then and only then do I let myself break.

Fingers curled around the steering wheel, head back against the headrest of the driver's seat, hot tears spill down my cheeks, and despite trying like hell to not let it, I feel the crack in my heart get bigger, until it shatters. The shitty thing in all of this is that despite having just broken my fucking heart, I still love the bastard.

That's okay though, because there is a fine line between love and hate, and as I wipe away the last of my tears, it's only a matter of time before one extreme becomes the other.

THIRTEEN

One Year Later

"**Y**OU HAVE TO stop moping, Klara. It's been a year since Braxton. You need to get out there again." Dri plops herself down on the sofa next to me. Her already short shorts riding up even higher.

"As much as I hate to agree with anything Adrienne says, I have to agree with her on this one. "It's time, Klara." I scoot over closer to Dri so that Rick can join us on the couch.

"It hasn't been that long," I scoff, crossing my arms under my chest knowing that they're probably right.

"It's been twelve months, hun." Dri rubs my back.

Okay, so maybe it has been that long, but I'm allowed to mope, aren't I? I mean, I did catch my – ugh, I don't even know what to call him—fucking some other chick in his office when we were supposed to be going for a lunch date.

"Look, Klara. We gave you six months, but when you still weren't over the prick we figured maybe you felt a little more for him than you were letting on, so we gave it more time to see if you would pull through it on your own. But enough is enough," Rick deadpans, glaring at me from over the rim of his beer bottle.

"And I did," I protest, not liking the fact that I seem to be outnumbered right now.

"No, babe, you didn't. You're just going through the motions. Work. Gym. And repeat. You haven't been out with us in a year, and you missed the Superbowl in Feb."

"Wait, what?" I turn to look at Rick. "I did? I missed the Superbowl? Who played? Who won?"

"See." Dri shakes her head. "This is what I mean. Before Braxton football was your life. You never missed a regular season game, let alone the Superbowl. You're not living, Klara. You're just existing."

Slumping back against the sofa, I sigh reaching for Dri's hand while laying my head on Rick's shoulder. "I thought I was doing okay. I thought I was holding it together. We weren't even together that long, for Christ's sake. Why is this so much harder?"

Dri snuggles in closer, resting her head on my shoulder, our hands still clasped together. "You know why," she sighs.

I did. Because I was in love with him. They would like to think it was just because I gave him my virginity, and maybe that was part of it. But I let myself get consumed by Braxton De Luca. I let him into my heart, even knowing that he had the potential to break it beyond repair.

I let out a shaky breath not wanting to argue with my two best friends at this moment. "I missed my birthday too, didn't I? And both of yours?"

They both nod, and I feel like the biggest fake friend. Rick leans the side of his head against mine, taking my other hand in his. "It's okay. You were hurting and we understood. But no more, Klara. I'm not going to stand by and watch while De Luca takes up more rent in that head of yours than he already has."

They're right, of course, but that doesn't make me any more eager to move on. If I was being honest with myself, I was hoping Braxton would come back. That he would realize he made a big mistake and would apologize profusely, beg me to take him back, and I would. Pathetic, huh? But entertaining that thought was easier than envisioning him with someone else. I wanted to be the one he came to for comfort at the end of a long day. I wanted to be the one who fell asleep in his arms, who got to enjoy his body. I wanted to be the one his eyes light up for. Not only am I pathetic, pining over a man who's probably already forgotten about me, but now I already hate the woman getting to hold him at night.

I glance up at Rick and then over at Dri. I can't put them through my mood swings any longer. If I don't want to move on for myself then I at least have to try for them.

"Okay." I give Dri's hand a squeeze and paste a smile on my face. "Set me up on one of those blind dates I know you've been dying to."

Her eyes round in shock when she sits up again, and I can't help the giggle that bubbles up because she looks like a cartoon character. "Are you serious right now? Don't play with me, Klara," she warns, but I see the gleam of hope in her eyes.

I nod, extracting myself from Rick. "I'm not playing. Do it. Set it up, Dri."

Adrienne fist pumps the air as she jumps up from the sofa and races to her room to presumably grab her laptop, or her phone, or whatever it is she does to set up these blind dates. Rick laughs to my side, the deep timber of his voice reverberating through my arm.

"I'm going to regret this, aren't I? Letting her set me up?"

Rick laughs harder, ruffling my hair as he gets up to replace his empty beer with a new one. "Have fun with that one," he calls over his shoulder. Our apartment door closes behind him as he retreats to his own apartment downstairs.

***

I'm going to kill my best friend. She's dead. Dead.

"You've got to be fucking kidding me," I mumble under my breath, willing myself to wake up from this nightmare. All the while, the driver's side door to the white sports car opens up—yes, up. Not out, because why wouldn't he flaunt his money at every possible opportunity—and out steps Mike Davis, because the universe couldn't be any crueler to me.

"You're my date? Adrienne set me up with you?" I bark, then insistently wince at the tone of my voice.

"Well, hello to you, too, stranger." He chuckles, holding open the door to the restaurant for me and ushering me inside.

"Is this some sick joke? I thought you were living in BC, working for the RCMP over there?"

Mike gives the hostess our name and we both watch as she goes to check if our table is ready. I must admit that he picked an excellent restaurant. They're known for their steak here, and if Mike's buying then I'm ordering a surf and turf.

"I do. I was just passing through on my way home from Europe when Dri texted."

Fucking Adrienne. She couldn't have waited one day. One day and Mike would've been on his way home to the other side of the country.

"You don't look so happy to see me, Gigs." He grins, ordering us two whiskeys, one on the rocks, from our waitress.

"Don't call me that." I glare at him, shifting uncomfortably in my seat.

I didn't have to come inside and sit down. I knew that I could've walked away the second I realized who Adrienne set me up with, but the thought of a free meal at his expense was just too tempting. Mike and I have a lot of history. A lot. Some of it was good, most of it not so much.

"You used to love when I called you that," he says, talking a sip of the drink our waitress just delivered to the table.

"I was a naïve teenager, and you were—"

"The bad boy you used to piss off your parents," he concludes, and I nod, swallowing past the lump in my throat.

Like I said, Mike and I have a lot of history. We were always skirting the boundaries, but never breeching them. Always playing with fire and hoping we never got burned. Until I did, and he left. Story of my fucking life. Silence envelopes us as we sit staring at each other, waiting for our food to arrive.

"Your hair's gotten longer," I point out.

He grins, running a hair through the shoulder length locks. "Backpacking around Europe for months will have that effect."

"I hate it," I blurt and inwardly cringe. What the hell was in that whiskey? I'm never this blunt, but then again it is Mike.

He chuckles. "Of course you do. Anything else not to your liking, your majesty?"

"Were you always such a sarcastic ass?"

"Were you always such a cold bitch?" he volleys back, and I flinch, pulling back the claws.

"I'm sorry." I sigh, taking another sip of my refilled drink. "It's been a tough year..."

Mike sits back in his seat, his eyes roaming over me. Shit, I used to hate when he got that look because I knew he knew that everything wasn't okay, and he would be right for the most part.

"Who's the guy?" he asks after a long stretched out silence.

"There is no guy," I snap, which only serves to strike his curiosity more.

"You mean there's no guy anymore."

"Mike." I let out a long breath, leaning back against the cool leather of the booth. "Can we not go there please?"

Our waitress brings our food, and I'm glad for the momentary relief from the questions I know will be volleyed at me the moment she leaves. I almost want to wrap my arms around her and beg her to stay, to sit with us and enjoy a break.

"Alright, Gigs. Spill."

I stop, fork halfway to my mouth with the juiciest piece of steak on it and narrow my eyes at him, but Mike just grins, mouth half full of steak and mashed potatoes, but that look in his eye tells me I'm not going to get away with dodging his questions as easily as I hoped. So, in between heavenly bites of steak, grilled veg, and creamy mashed potatoes—I didn't go with the surf and turf—I tell him all about Braxton.

At the end of it all, it feels like a huge weight has been lifted from my shoulders. But now it's been almost twenty minutes and Mike hasn't said a word, of which I was grateful for while I was telling my sob story, but it's a little unnerving now.

Instead of making digs at me like I suspected he would, Mike effortlessly changes the subject, and before I know it we're actually laughing and talking like old friends again, and I'm almost sad to see him go after our date ends.

With his hand against my lower back, Mike leads me out of the restaurant after paying our bill and gives the valet attendant his ticket.

"I'm sorry for leaving the way I did," he says, turning to me.

"We were kids. I shouldn't have gone off on you like that. Just with everything that happened with Braxton, it was easier to still be mad at you."

"Still, Klara. You needed me after what happened with your parents, and instead of sticking by you like a best friend should, I tucked tail and ran. They were like parents to me, but they were your parents, and I should've been there. I'm sorry, Gigs." He pulls me into his arms as fresh tears pool in my eyes.

"I'm glad we did this, even if it was a blind date."

Mike laughs. "Remind me to never let Adrienne set me up again." He pulls away but still keeps his hands on my shoulders.

"Deal, and ditto."

The valet pulls up in Mike's car, but he lingers a bit longer not making a move to let go of my shoulders. "He loves you," he says, his voice low, a hint of sadness and longing in his eyes before he blinks it away.

"Braxton doesn't love me," I scoff. "I was nothing more than a new shiny toy."

Mike shakes his head, taking a step back. "He did what I never could with Kirsten. He loved you enough to let you go."

My heart pangs at the mention of Mike's ex-girlfriend who was now living on the other side of the world with her new husband and baby. There was a point where we thought we were going to lose Kirsten. After Mike finished his RCMP training and got stationed on the west coast in British Columbia, Kirsten was caught in a bank robbery and had been shot. Mike had taken on all the guilt since he was supposed to have been at the bank appointment and not her. I know a part of him wished he had left her to keep her safe from his line of work when he got accepted onto the elite team, but he just couldn't let her go. Then, when the brother of the man he put down came after him and his team, they kidnapped Kirsten. Luckily, Mike and his team got to her in time, but Kirsten wasn't able to do it anymore, so she left him.

"Mike—"

Mike steps into me, pulling me into another hug and effectively cutting me off. We hug again before he lets go. "You sure you don't want a ride?"

"No." I tip my head to the side. "It's rare that I get to walk anymore, and it's a nice night out. I'll be okay."

Mike nods. "You'll be okay, Gigs. You're stronger than you think you are." Then he disappears inside the car as it roars to life a few seconds later and takes off.

I may have wanted to murder Adrienne when I first saw who she set me up with, but now I just want to hug her and thank her. Somehow, she knew that Mike was the one I needed to talk to. After all, he was the one I went to when we were in high school and I needed to talk. They both told it to me straight, never once beating around the bush, but Adrienne knew that despite what she said, Mike always had a way of getting through to me what she couldn't. She never resented him for it, it was just the way our threesome worked.

It stung a little that I couldn't have all three of my best friends with me, but I knew the city life was never for Mike. He needed to be on the coast, where he could escape to the open water if the need ever arose. And honestly, it sounded like he was thriving on the west coast in B.C.

Me: Thank you for tonight. I never realized how badly I needed it until now.

Mike: Anytime, Gigs. Don't be a stranger. I miss you.

Me: You better not be texting and driving *angry face*

Mike: You were always cute when you tried to frown. But alas, I am not driving anymore. I'm safely back at my hotel until morning. Are you home yet?

Me: Just walked through the door. Goodnight, Trouble.

Mike: Goodnight, Gigs.

113

FOURTEEN

Six Months Later

I **STILL SEE** Braxton everywhere. In the streets of the city we explored together. In the café where he first tracked me down. At the gym where I work. I feel his eyes tracking my every movement, from the moment I leave my apartment building 'til the moment I return. I see his black coupe driving by when I go for my morning run, I see it parked down side-streets.

I see him in strangers I walk by. In men leaving work at the end of the day. He's everywhere and nowhere all at once. I can't get him out of my head, and it's driving me mad.

"You shouldn't be walking these streets this late by yourself."

I stop a few steps away from the door to my apartment building. Gio is standing with his back to the building, a foot propped on it, arms crossed over his chest.

"What are you doing here? Did Braxton send you?"

I have so many questions. I want to know how he's been. What he's been up to the last eighteen months. If there's anything new in his life, but I don't ask any of it because I'm afraid of the answers. I'm afraid Gio will tell me Braxton is doing great, that he's already moved on and forgotten about me.

"He doesn't." Gio flicks a cigarette down I hadn't seen when I first walked up and stomps it out on the sidewalk. "And would you believe me if I said that I missed having you around the house?" He looks up at me sheepishly, his lips twitching.

"You missed me, or my baking?" I ask, one eyebrow raised.

He chuckles, running a hand over the back of his neck. "Both? Braxton's ma, she's good with food, not so good with chocolate and pastries." He pauses, placing a hand over his belly. "And you know how much I love my sweets."

I giggle, looking him over and then down the street before cutting my gaze back. "And he didn't send you?"

"He doesn't know I'm here, Klara."

I wanted his voice to soothe me. Braxton hadn't sent him. I was allowed to continue healing and move on. But they did the opposite of soothe because yes, while I did want to grieve him and move on, I also wanted him to fight for us, even if I didn't know what he was supposed to be fighting. I still don't understand why we can't be together. His excuses were vague. I sigh, and that's what it comes down to, they were just excuses. But I'm okay. I will be okay. I've already made it this far without him.

"Alright." I motion for Gio to follow me through the door to the building.

I spent the rest of the night making the chocolate candies Gio loved so much. It really wasn't that hard. Just some melted chocolate chips and sweetened condensed milk mixed together and left in the fridge until hard then cut into bite size pieces. They were really closer to fudge than anything but Gio loved them and it was nice to hang out with him again.

After hours upon hours of Full House reruns, enough chocolate to make the Easter bunny jealous, and a few shots of whiskey, Gio reluctantly left at almost two in the morning, and my heart broke all over again because I knew that once Braxton found out Gio was still hanging around me, he would shit a brick. And he would find out, it was just a matter of time.

***

The sound of my phone pinging with a new message rouses me from a shitty sleep. After Gio left early this morning I moved from the couch to my bed, not bothering to get into it but passing out on top of the covers.

Those shots of whiskey are not looking like the greatest idea this morning though. My head is pounding and my mouth feels like a giant cotton ball. My phone pings again and I groan at the loud noise and bright screen.

Brax: I miss you.

Brax: I'm sorry.

Is he for real right now? He can't just text me after almost two years and think I'm going to drop everything and text him back. I refuse to be at his beck and call.

"Klara! Are you up?" Dri pounds on my bedroom and I want to kill her. For the briefest moment, I contemplate killing my best friend, and who I could enlist to help dump her body.

"Klara?" She calls again through the closed door, and it feels like a jackhammer hammering through my scalp.

"Yeah," I groan, feeling the whiskey threaten a return journey. I'm never drinking that much again. What the hell was wrong with me last night that I thought going shot for shot with Gio was a good idea? I should've known he could drink me under the table. Damn those Italian men and their alcohol resistance.

"Good morning, sunshine," Dri singsongs, pushing open my door and jumping onto the foot of the bed.

"Dri." I groan, trying to breathe through the nausea.

"Late night?" She giggles.

"The fuck are you so cheery at too-damn-early in the morning?" I side eye her as another text comes through.

Brax: I don't deserve your forgiveness, Klara. But fuck, I want to spend the rest of my life earning it. I'm sorry, baby.

I swallow past the lump forming in my throat. I never would have taken Braxton De Luca as the groveling type. But groveling is what he seems to be doing. Too bad it's two years too late. Or is it? Stop it, Klara. I am not going back to him. He can shove it.

"Klara, are you listening?"

I sigh, turning the volume off and putting the phone face down on my nightstand before turning to my best friend. "I'm sorry, Dri. Work email," I lie, hoping she bought it.

Dri goes back to telling me about her night with Matt, and then I spend the rest of the day getting the apartment ready for the upcoming week while simultaneously trying to keep my mind off Braxton.

By the time I crawl back into bed for the night, I'm physically exhausted from the grueling workout I put it through, and the abundance of chores I forced myself to do. But no matter how hard I scrubbed the bathroom or kitchen, or how much laundry I did, or how many little odds and ends I dusted, Braxton was never far from my mind.

FIFTEEN

THE COVERS ARE ripped from my body, the cold air from the air conditioner hitting my exposed limbs. Cold hands grab at my arms, and I know instantly that they don't belong to Braxton or Dri. Even though there was no reason for Braxton to come back. He had made it clear that I was nothing to him but an itch to scratch, a curiosity that needed to be explored. I stupidly gave him my heart and got nothing but rejection in its place.

No, these were not Braxton De Luca's hands. These hands were cold, bruising. I fight through the veil of fatigue plaguing my body and struggle against the intruder's grip when two more grab my ankles holding me down until the first set of hands pull me up and against a male body.

"Fucking take the damn picture already," a heavy accented voice says behind my ear. "Fuck, she feels so good. No wonder De Luca was so obsessed with her."

My stomach drops at the sound of Braxton's name. No, there was no way he was part of this. Braxton claimed that he was a monster but he would never hurt me. It was one of the excuses he gave when he ripped my heart out. "Don't want this evil life to touch you, Mia Bella." I still didn't know what he did for work. He was very skilled in keeping that part of his life hidden from me, carefully avoiding answering my questions.

The second man chuckles, but it's a dark, sinister sound. "He'll wish he died alongside the bitch after we're through with him."

"No! let me go!" I scream, hoping our neighbors hear me, but nobody comes, and I struggle harder, putting my all into jamming an elbow and heel back in hopes that one of them connects with my kidnapper.

"Fuck! Did you take it already? I'm going to knock this bitch out."

My elbow connects with a fleshy side causing my captor's breath to leave in a whoosh and his hands loosen around me for a second but it's not long enough to wiggle free.

"For fuck sakes, G. Knock her ass out already," man number one barks.

"I'm trying. Hold her still. Don't want to accidentally get you."

That voice. I recognize that voice, but it can't be. He was supposed to be my friend, my confidant.

The man holding me grunts, his arms tightening around me, squeezing the breath out of my lungs. Then I feel the prick in my neck, and suddenly my limbs grow heavy and I have to fight to keep my eyes open but eventually my vision fades to black, and everything around me disappears. The last thing on my mind being Braxton and how I wish he was here.

My savior. My dark knight.

PART 2

ONE

BRAXTON

"**OUT. GET OUT!**"

"But, Sir."

"Get the fuck out!" I roar at my receptionist, pushing up from my seat behind the marble desk. I can hear the blood pumping through my veins, can feel the white-hot anger coursing through my body.

Gone.

She's gone.

There one minute, and not the next.

The picture on my phone now seared into my memory. Klara, in tiny sleep shorts and a barely there tank top, eyes wild and full of fear. Her body forced back into the body of the masked kidnapper with their gloved hand covering her screams. A telltale bruise already forming on her delicate skin. My blood boils, the beast inside of me rattling the cage, demanding to be let free.

Reaching an arm out, I swipe everything off my desk in one move and then run a shaking hand through my hair.

Fuck! I looked away for five damn minutes, but that was all they needed to snatch her up from under me. Five goddamn minutes and everything I loved in this ugly world was taken from me.

Nausea rolls through me and I have to stumble back into the rolling office chair behind me before I lose my equilibrium.

Klara.

Beautiful, full of life Klara. Sweet and innocent and untouched by this life, until I got my filthy paws on her. I told her I was no good for her. I told her I would ruin her, that I would make her wish she had never laid eyes on me. I told her that I was the monster her parents warned her about.

She didn't believe me. She never did. She would scoff, lay her hand over my heart and say, "I believe there's good in you, Brax."

Silly girl should've listened when I told her I was no good for her. That this life would destroy her. And if I didn't find her and get her back, it would surely kill her.

I will kill the fuckers that dare lay a hand on what's mine. I may have walked away from her to save her from this very scenario but make no mistake that Klara Blouin is and will always been mine. I will rip them limb from limb with my bare hands. They wanted to see Braxton De Luca break. Well prepare yourself, motherfuckers, because I just fucking broke.

Visions of her pale blue eyes widened in shock float through my mind. The last time I saw my beautiful

Klara I pushed her away, convinced she couldn't love a monster like me. I was convinced I could not bring her into this lifestyle. She walked into my office for our scheduled lunch date and saw exactly what I wanted her to see. Me balls deep in my then assistant. I fired that bitch the minute Klara turned tail and ran like she couldn't get away from me fast enough.

I wanted to kick my own ass for the horrified expression that marred her beautiful face, but like the asshole I am, I put my dick back in my pants, fired the whore who tried getting into my pants from the second she was hired, shut the steel walls in place, and went on to torture another associate who thought he could play me, the Don, the head of the fucking mafia.

But like a fucking addict, I couldn't get Klara out of my head. I've had Gio and Alessandro keeping tabs on her every move for almost two years, and whenever time allowed, I would be the one watching her.

My beautiful Klara was so broken for that first year. Barely ever leaving her apartment for several months, always scanning the streets when she did. I knew she was looking for me. Looking to see if I would magically appear again. Even after what I did to her, she still held out hope that I would go back to her. And fuck, did I want to.

One year after the incident in my office, she went on her first date, and it took everything in me to not rip the bastard to pieces. The beast in me wanted to drag her away and claim her as mine, but fuck, I couldn't. I would not be the reason for the life to dim in her eyes.

That was the shit of it though, wasn't it? Because for almost a full year, I was the reason why she was holed up in her apartment, barely a shell of the person she was.

"Boss."

Antonio, my best friend since childhood, strolls into my office, followed closely by Alessandro, my second-in-command and the Capo Bastone of our famiglia.

"You'll get her back, Brax," Antonio says, handing me a tumbler of whiskey.

"Yeah, Boss. Already got Soldiers on it. There isn't a place on this earth where they can hide and we won't find them. They're good as dead." Alessandro crosses his arms in front of his chest and scowls at me, his eyes going from grey to black as the darkest night.

I nod and down the whiskey in a single gulp. It doesn't surprise me that these two are here without me calling them and telling them about the picture on my phone that had my blood running cold. I trust these men with my life, they're my brothers, my famiglia. Blood may not connect us, but death brought us together. And they are the only ones I trust with helping me bring Klara home. They're the only ones I trust with her life.

"Has Gio traced the number that sent the message?" My voice is hoarse, rough. And I try like hell to get a hold of myself. I can't fall apart now. Not when my woman needs me more than ever. I'm supposed to be the fucking Don. I mentally slap myself at the same time I refill the glass tumbler in my hand.

Alessandro tips his chin in a slight nod. "They're waiting for you."

I down a second refill of the whiskey, wiping my mouth with the back of my hand. "It's showtime, boys."

Alessandro's grin is sinister. He fucking lives for this stuff. For the thrill of the chase, the reward of the blood that will inevitably flow, the power of the kill. He's the kind of man you want working for you, not against you. He's the monster you pray doesn't come after you in the middle of the night. But Alessandro, he still doesn't have anything on me.

I'm the thing the monster is afraid of.

I'm the thing the worst nightmares are made of.

"Boss." Gio nods as soon as we step foot into the concrete basement thirty minutes later.

You'd never know this room was here. A torture chamber of sorts in the middle of downtown. It was part of the reason why I bought this building and had them make the basement fully concrete with extra sound proofing... just in case. The other reason being that the building was not purchased in my name. The one and only thing purchased in my name were the small block of offices holding my financial company upstairs. If by chance things were to go south and this basement was to be considered, it would never trace back to me. Lesson number one my father had taught me.

"What do we have here?" I ask, eyeing the already bloody man tied to a chair in the middle of the dark room.

"Number that sent that picture is in his name."

"P-Please. I don't know what you're talking about. I d-d-didn't send no picture," he stutters, pulling on his restraints.

He thinks pleading to my humanity might save him from his fate. It's almost laughable really. There's no humanity fucking left in me. There hasn't been for a long time.

"Shut up!" Gio roars, his fist connecting with the man's jaw.

I stand back and watch the scene play out before me, but the more Gio lays into him, the more he insists he didn't send a picture, that he has no idea about a girl.

"Enough of this!" I bellow, and all movement in the room stops. I size up the man sitting hunched forward in the chair, blood pouring from the various wounds on his face, his eyes swelling shut, and then to Gio. Casually, I slide my hands into the pockets of my designer suit pants and shrug. "No need to keep him around if he doesn't know anything then. Finish it," I command then turn to let Gio and Alessandro have their fun.

"Wait! Wait! S-Someone, a man, came into my store and asked to use the phone. The store phone was down so I let him use my cell. P-Please, that's all I know," the man begs.

All breathing ceases in the room, and I can feel three pairs of eyes on me as I turn back to the bloody mess. If he thinks he can play me with that bullshit excuse and I'll let him walk then he has another thing coming. "Do you have a description of this man?"

He nods violently. I'm almost afraid he's going to break his neck before my boys will have the chance.

I nod at Alessandro. "Get the description." I pause. "Then finish it, but make it quick. Ma is expecting us at the dinner table tonight."

"W-What, why? I... Please don't kill me."

127

"Would love to, but you're collateral damage." I shrug and then exit the room.

***

"Ma, let me do that," I scold my mother and reach for the heavy dish in her hands. Out of the corner of my eye I catch Gio and Alex – Alessandro – sneak into the dining room in hopes that my mother didn't notice they were late.

I smirk, knowing that she noticed because very little gets by my mother.

"Giovanni Russo and Alessandro Ferrara, you better have washed up before sitting down at my dinner table." My mother eyes both men.

"Wouldn't've dared not to, Mrs. De Luca," Gio supplies for the both of them.

Dinner goes off without a hitch. Ma's cooking, as always, is spectacular, and if I wasn't about to hop on a plane I would've had a second—or third—helping. But I know my boys are sitting on the information I need to get one step closer to finding my girl and bringing her home.

When we're done, the three of us help Ma bring the plates back to the kitchen, despite all her protests, then we each kiss her on the cheek and head back to my office.

"Well?" I stalk toward the wet bar and pour myself a healthy glass of whiskey. I don't offer a drink to the men standing behind me. They know they can get their own drink them-damn-selves. I'm not their servant.

"You're not going to like this Braxton." Gio shifts from one foot to the other.

My name used to grate on my nerves. I'm the only one in the famiglia with an English first name and an Italian last name. Braxton didn't fit.

But somehow, when it was leaving Klara's lips while I pounded into her, that was the only time I didn't mind it. Fucking loved it, actually. I sigh, taking a seat behind my desk and run a hand through my hair.

"Well, stop pussy-footing and get to it."

Alessandro's gaze turns cold, his hands clenching into fists at his sides. "It was one of Dante's men."

"The fuck did you just say?"

"The one who sent the picture of Klara. It was one of Dante's men."

The whiskey I just drank turns sour in the pit of stomach. Fuck me, if it was true and Dante really did have Klara, she could be anywhere in the fucking world by now. It had barely been twenty-four hours since she was taken, but that didn't mean shit in our world. If Dante meant for her to disappear, then disappear she would. At least until her body showed up months, maybe even years later.

Dante was one sick fuck. But that didn't surprise me in the least, because he was my cousin. An estranged cousin, but a cousin nonetheless.

"You sure?"

Both men tip their chin in a nod. "I'd bet my life on it," Gio adds.

"What do you want to do, Boss?" Alessandro asks after several beats of silence.

My answer was automatic. I didn't have to think about it. There was no way I was going to let Klara go without a fight. Without even trying to find her. Fuck that. I would find her. And there'll be hell to pay for any fucker stupid enough to get in my way. Blood or not. They say that the road to hell is paved with good intentions. My cousin and his men better get ready, because they're on a one-way trip to hell. My hell.

The beast inside me was calm whenever Klara was around, and now with her gone he was pacing the confines of his cage just itching for me to budge an inch. An inch was all he needed to escape. Fuck, I might let him out to play anyway.

"We go get her."

THE CLUB MY cousin owns is a warehouse in the west end of Toronto. By the looks of the outside, you would never guess that beyond the steel door is pristine, upper class—read: invite only—nightclub. Crystal chandeliers hang from the ceiling in various lengths, blood red velvet curtains separate the VIP rooms from the dance floor. When the lights are off, save for the strobe lights, the entire place is cast in darkness. Shadows. The white dance floor in the middle of the dark stone floor the only beacon of light.

It's just enough to put you at ease as any other nightclub would, while still being overly aware of the monster lurking in the shadows.

Fitting. Considering who owns the club and just how fucked up our family really is.

"Club doesn't open for several hours, boys. You'll have to come back then."

My eyes rake up the scrawny man standing a few feet in front of us. Either he's a new in town, or has a fucking death wish. Everyone in this city knows who I am.

A snarl sounds to my right, and I hold up my hand, never breaking eye contact with the shit in front of me, to stop Gio from pushing forward and ending this punk's life too soon.

"Do you know who I am?" I ask with a smirk.

"No, and I don't care. Like I said, club doesn't open for several hours. You're welcome to come back then."

The kid pivots on his heel and goes to walk away. He doesn't get far when both Gio and Alessandro jump into action. Each grabbing an arm, Alessandro pushes the kid's face into the newly cleaned surface of the bar.

Rolling up the sleeves of my black dress shirt, I take a stand on the other side of the bar, eyeing the various liquor bottles on the wall in front of me until they land on the most expensive whiskey my cousin has to offer.

I take my time reaching for a crystal tumbler and pouring myself a couple fingers worth of the rich, amber liquid. Enjoying the way the little shit is squirming under Alessandro's bruising hold.

I down the first drink, and pour another. "You know, I had intended on only coming in here to see if my cousin had made an appearance today, but then you had to go and disrespect me."

He stops squirming and visible pales under the strong hand holding him in place. "Y-You're Braxton De Luca."

"Ah, so you have heard of me." I tip the tumbler in a cheers gesture before bringing it to my lips. Fuck, I love watching people's reactions when they realize that they fucked up, and could very nearly pay with their lives. All because of a stupid mistake.

"Look, man, I'm sorry. Fuck, I'm new here and didn't realize who you were."

There was very little our famiglia wouldn't do. Not a line we wouldn't cross for the right amount of money, or power. Hell, or both. After all, with money comes power. But what I couldn't stand? What I had very little patience for, was anyone hurting women and children, and disrespect.

I don't care who you are, if you disrespect me, my family, or anyone I know chances are you won't be leaving our encounter with all your limbs intact, and if you really cross me I won't think twice about taking your life.

I tip my chin in a nod and watch as Gio and Alessandro flip the kid onto his back over the bar, his head mere inches from the edge.

"You disrespected me once and I let it slide. But then you went and disrespected me again, man." I emphasize the word, letting him know exactly where he went horribly wrong. "And that... that I just can't let slide."

Alessandro's big hand presses down on the boy's forehead effectively tipping his chin up at the same time Gio holds his arms down and my fingers wrap around the glass bottle.

"Time for a lesson in respect. I expect you to listen up and pay attention, because there'll be a quiz after." I pinch his nose closed with one hand, forcing his mouth to open, and with the other tip the head of the bottle down causing a stream of the golden liquid. "Lesson one. Never fucking call me man. It's Sir, or Mr. De Luca."

I tip the bottle back, stopping the flow, and release my hold on his nose. He sputters and chokes trying to fight off the grip on his forehead and the ones pinning him in place.

"Are you ready for your second and final lesson?" I ask.

"No. Fuck, no, I'm so sorry. I'll never—"

His pleas get cut off when my name is hollered from the VIP curtains to my right.

"Braxton!"

That voice. It's been years, but I'll never forget the sound of that voice. The clacking of her heels against the stone floor add to my growing irritation.

"You never did know how to play nice," she says, coming to stop at my side. Her flowery scent swirling around me.

There was a time when I would've had her back pressed into the wall, my cock buried so deep inside her that she wouldn't be able to speak for interrupting my business like the way she just had. But now, now my cock barely takes notice of her anymore. Might have something to do with her leaving me for my fucking cousin two days before our wedding day.

"And you never did know how to mind your own fucking business, Amanda."

"Ah, but see…" She shifts closer, running one long manicured finger down my bicep. "This kind of is my business. I'm part owner of this club, Luca, and he is one of my employees."

"Not for long," I growl, turning back to my previous task but Amanda sidles up against me, pushing her fake tits into my arm, while her fingers roam down my pecs.

My fingers wrap around the wrist of her roaming hand and I spin, backing her into the wall of liquor bottles so hard that the sound of glass shattering echoes around us. But Amanda grins, bucking her hips into mine.

"Always did like it rough," she purrs, and I snarl baring my teeth.

"Cut the shit, Amanda. Where's Dante?"

"Not here." A long leg wraps around my hip. "I've missed you, Luca. I've missed having you throw me around like this and then fuck me senseless. I miss this big…" her other hand reaches down and squeezes my limp cock, "dick," she pants.

I grip her other wrist, cutting off her hold on me and raise both her hands above her head. "He's not in the mood for whore pussy right now," I growl, satisfied when my hit lands and anger flames behind her dark eyes. Eyes as dark as her fucking heart.

"What, you get a taste of virgin pussy and all of a sudden you forget who you are? You forget what makes you fucking you."

I move fast. Fingers curling around her throat, both hands bound together in one of mine and then I let a little of the beast show. "Where is she?"

Amanda stills, nostrils flaring, her chest raising fast with her heavy breathing. "She's not here. Dante wouldn't say where he was taking her. Just that she would make him the most money. The best for his best buyers."

Despite her claims, Amanda never could handle all of me. She could handle the Don, but the beast was darker, more violent, he had a penchant for the taste of blood. I know she would sing if I gave her a glimpse of what was hiding beneath the surface.

It wasn't lost on me that I had officially come full circle. I was standing in the very club where I first met Klara, watching her on the dance floor and wondering what it would take for me to convince her to leave with me that night. Now, I was standing here looking for her. Wondering what it would take for me to get her back in my arms. Where she belongs. And safe.

"Where's your husband, Amanda?" I demand, my fingers tightening around her delicate throat. I can feel her pulse beat rapidly beneath my fingers, and it only serves to feed my need for blood.

"I-I don't... please, Braxton, you're choking me," she wheezes, her wrists rolling under my grip trying to break free.

My grip around her throat tightens even more while I run the tip of my nose up her jaw. "Thought you said you liked when I got rough. Missed it even."

Her lips part as she struggles to take in breath after breath, her eyes widening in fear. I know if I add a little more pressure it'll be damn near impossible for her breathe and after a several seconds her body will start to go limp. My fingers twitch with my indecision. The beast is growling, wanting me to end her, to satisfy the craving momentarily. But the man knows that without her Dante will be in the wind and I need to track him down if I have any hope of bringing Klara home alive.

Frustrated by my indecision, I abandon my grip around her wrists and yank her forward before shoving her back against the glass again. Her head bouncing off the cracks, her eyes momentarily closing when I run a hand down the side of her face even while the grip around her throat doesn't waver.

"Where is he, Amanda? Not going to ask again. You've already tested my patience."

She claws at my arms, her fake nails leaving little scratches in their wake. "I don't—"

"Boss," Alessandro interrupts. I mentally shake myself. I had forgotten that we weren't along in the club, and that they had the punk who worked here bent over the bar. I hadn't heard a sound out of them so I'm assuming Gio or Alessandro knocked the kid out.

"What!" I bark, never turning my eyes away from Amanda.

"Word on the street is Dante went into hiding after hearing you were on your way here."

"Pussy," Gio mumbles under his breath and my lips twitch in a smirk.

My cousin never did have any balls when it came to confronting me or me him. If he got word that I was pissed and looking to take it out on him, he would go running until something else distracted me and the coast was clear. Seems like nothing has changed, except this time there would be no distractions, and I won't be stopping until my concrete floor runs red with his blood and anyone else who got between me and Klara.

"Get all the soldiers on it. I want every fucking inch of this city searched, and I want to know the minute he emerges or if he leaves."

Footsteps sound behind me and I assume that they belong to Gio or Alessandro going to deliver my instructions, the other staying behind in case I needed them.

"What do you want to do with them, Boss?" Gio asks meaning Amanda and the kid.

"Let the kid go."

I wait until the sound of shuffling feet disappears, my eyes still trained on the bitch in front of me.

"You can't…kill…me. Deep down… you still… love me." She's growing weak from the lack of oxygen, struggling to get words out.

It would bring me immense pleasure to end her life right here, right now. To see the life leave her eyes. To hit my cousin where it hurts the most. Apparently, my rule about women and children did not extend to her.

"Ah, see that's where you're wrong, Puttana." Her eyes widen at the use of that name directed at her. I grin enjoying watching her squirm, watching her reactions to this darker side of me that I kept hidden around her. "I don't love you. In fact, I'm trying real hard not to kill you. Do you want to die, Amanda?"

Her hands ball into fists against my chest and she tries to shove me away, but her attempts are laughable.

"Let me go, Braxton." Tears pool in the depths of her eyes, and I'm the sick bastard who takes great joy in making her cry.

"Do you want to die, Amanda?" I repeat my question, lips brushing her ear, voice cold. "Do you want to feel my blade slice through this throat like butter? Do you want to feel the life slowly leave your body? Hmm?"

"No," she sobs. "Please…" she begs.

I slam her back further into the wall. "Good. Tell my fucking cousin I'm looking for him and not to leave town. If he does, Amanda, I'll be back, and you'll be paying with your life," I growl in front of her face. "Don't make me come back here, yeah?"

I feel her throat working to swallow beneath my fingers as she nods frantically, promising that she'll do whatever I say. I leave her to slide down the wall in a crying mess as I nod toward Gio who had come back not too long ago and casually slide my hands into the pockets of my dress pants making my way out the club and back to my car.

Usually I would wait out my prey. Wait for them to emerge from their hiding place, but not this time. Waiting could cost Klara her life. My chest aches with the thought of never seeing her again. Never hearing the bite of her tongue when she calls me out on my bullshit. No, I would not be waiting. This time I was going to smoke out my prey, and when he finally emerged from his hole, I would be in the shadows... waiting, ready to strike.

THREE

I'M GOING CRAZY. Losing my shit.

It's been a week since Klara was taken and my damn cousin is still in hiding, nobody has seen or heard from him since he got word that I was on my way to his club to track him down. Loosening the tie around my neck, I gulp down the rest of the bourbon in the crystal tumbler between my fingers and immediately pour a refill. Not caring in the least that bourbon fucks with my head more than any other liquor.

One week. Seven days. One-hundred-sixty-eight hours. Over ten-thousand minutes.

My fingers tighten around the glass until my knuckles turn white and then it's hurdling through the air until the sound of glass shattering sounds against the far wall of my office. I run my hands through my hair, gripping the ends, wanting to tear it out. I haven't slept in seven days. Refused to eat more than the minimum to just keep me alive, spending hours upon hours at the office gym downstairs or the one I'd had built in my house.

I can't even walk into my fucking house without seeing her face. So trusting. So full of life. And I fucked it up by bringing her into this life. She wasn't supposed to be anything other than a one-night fuck in the back office of the club. But she turned my life upside down. Made me crave her in ways I didn't know was possible.

"Boss," Alessandro knocks, pushing open the heavy wood door to my office. I don't bother looking up, knowing that what he will see will be a man, made weak by the woman he loves.

Loves? The fuck?

I don't do love. I can't do love in my line of work because shit like this happens and fucks with my head. I've already put important matters on the back burner so that I can focus all my attention on getting this girl back.

Guilt.

I feel guilt for bringing her into this mess, that's all. I'm going to fix it by bringing her home and then I'll wash my hands of the situation after making sure she's safe. Braxton De Luca does not do love. Fuck that shit. Love is for the weak.

"Got one of Dante's associates in the basement. Got a tip he may know where Dante is."

Carefully schooling my features and taking a deep breath, I look up at Alessandro and nod. I follow him out a moment later, rolling up the sleeves of my shirt and getting ready to do business.

***

I'm hidden by the shadows in the basement watching as Gio takes jumper cables to the guy's fingers. I'm not one of those men who runs an empire but refuse to get dirty. I still thrive on the blood... the death that comes with this life, but Alessandro sensed that my mind wasn't in the game and suggested I watch from the shadows for now. On a normal day, he would've gotten my blade for making such a suggestion. I never asked my men to do what I was not prepared to do myself. But nothing about this week has been normal. Reluctantly, I agreed which shocked the shit out of not just him but myself too.

So here I stand. Leaning a shoulder against the far wall basked in shadows. Hands casually resting in my dress pants. The picture of cool, calm, and collected while I watch my two best men torture my cousin's whereabouts out of this man. Meanwhile, there's a war raging inside me. A beast rattling its cage, looking for that one weak spot so it can finally break free of its chains.

There are times when I wonder if the roles were reversed, if I were the one strapped to that chair getting the ever-loving shit beat out of me, would I talk as easily as everyone who has ever sat there has? Or would I welcome death? Would I embrace my fate? Laugh in its face? Would I struggle against my restraints and my captors? Would I fight, the way I hope Klara has, to stay alive?

The simple answer? No, I wouldn't fight. I'd welcome the end with open arms. I've done enough, seen enough in this life. I scrub a hand down my face. If I ever had the choice, I would walk away from it all.

I scoff. Yeah, thirty-three fucking years of this shit and given half a chance I would walk away with no regrets. I would leave it all behind without a backward glance.

But a choice, there is not. I was born into this life and the only way I was leaving it was by death.

Gio looks to me in silent approval to up the ante on the man strapped to the chair, and I nod, not giving a shit what lengths he has to go to get the information we need. Fuck, start chopping off limbs for all I care. I just need him alive long enough to give me what I want.

Savage? Sure.

Ruthless? Maybe.

Necessity? Fuck yeah. Anything to bring Klara home.

"You're wasting your time. I don't know where Dante is, and even if I did, I wouldn't tell you." He spits blood at Gio's feet and I see the moment Gio shuts down, the moment his demons come to the surface to play, but I have to shut that shit down before he kills the little fuck.

Wielding the gator machete over one shoulder, I make my way out of the shadows keeping my head down until I'm standing in front of the man strapped to the chair and slowly, menacingly I lift my eyes to his, smirking when the first real sign of fear flashes behind his eyes.

Gio and Alessandro eye the knife over my shoulder and wisely take a step back without another word or protest. I've had enough of this amateur shit. It was time to let the beast out to play.

"Tell me, how much do you think your life is worth?"

He squirms in his seat, trying to move as far back from me as he physically can while his hands and feet are strapped to the frame of the chair, and I let him. There's nowhere for him to go. Nowhere for him to hide. Eventually, everyone's darkest nightmare catches up with them.

"Do you value your life?" I ask stalking toward him like a predator to its prey.

Fear is a funny thing. Wield it right and it can be the best motivator. But wield it wrong, and it can be the worst paralyzer. I can practically smell the fear emanating from his pores, can hear the blood rushing through his veins, see his pulse rapidly beating in his neck.

"Answer the question," I bark.

"Go to hell." He breathes out hard. Steeling his chin and forcing himself to not retreat again when I step closer.

I hold my hands out to the side in a look-around-you gesture. "I'm already here." I bring the fifteen-inch fine-edge side of the blade down the side and across, slicing through both shins.

"Ah, fuuuck!"

My smirk turns into a full grin when his screams reach my ears and as I watch the blood flow down his legs. Yes, I'm a sick bastard, but he should know not to get between me and what I want.

I spend the next hour delivering little slices with my blade and watching as his blood pools beneath the chair and runs toward the drain in the middle of the concrete floor. He's fading in and out of consciousness now so I kick his chair hard enough to jostle him.

"Give me what I want and all this stops."

His head falls forward, chin resting against his chest, his eyes fighting to stay open. "You'll just kill me anyway." His voice is weak, barely audible in the cold basement. Alessandro walks behind him, gripping his hair and pulling his head up so that I can see his face.

"Tell me what I want to know and I may spare you."

"And waste my last breath trying to appeal to the De Luca humanity that doesn't exist? I'd rather choose death."

I look over my shoulder at Gio and nod, turning back to the fucker strapped to my chair as Gio hands me a used leather wallet. I hoped that he would've told me what I want to hear before it ever came down to this but this little fuck is like a stone wall. I pull out the wrinkled paper, eyeing the smiling family in the picture.

"If you don't value your own life, what of that of your wife? Your kids?"

New life sparks behind his eyes, adrenaline fueled raged causing the fight back in him. "You sonuva bitch! Leave my family alone," he snarls.

"Alessandro, where's the wife now?"

"Just finishing up her weekly yoga class, Boss. Bitch looked good enough to eat in those damn yoga pants." He grins, tightening his hold around the fucker's hair.

"You sick fuck!" He spits, struggling against Alessandro's hold and his binds.

"Tell me what I want to know and I'll make sure Alessandro here doesn't go near your precious wife."

His shoulders hunch forward, all fight leaving his tired and weak body. "She's supposed to be in a shipping container bound for Cuba tonight. Dante is scheduled to be there, too."

I look to Alessandro and Gio in a silent command to clean this shit up before making my way toward the basement stairs. "Dump his body where they'll find it in the morning." Stopping before I reach the door I add,

"Leave the wife alone…for now." Then push open the door and step out of hell.

***

(Klara)

I wake up in a daze. I'm freezing, goosebumps litter my arms and legs, but I can't cover them because my hands are still bound behind me back. My shoulder ache from being stretched behind me for hours. I need to pee, but unless I want to embarrass myself I know I have to hold it. I just don't know for how long.

Muffled voices sound outside the metal container and I shift a little to try and get closer to the crack in the door so that I can hear them better.

"Rueben's dead. They found his body this morning. Blade wounds."

"He's getting closer."

"Should we move the girl?"

Muffled curses and then silence.

"Did he tell them what we said to?"

"He held his own until De Luca threatened the wife. Told him she was being shipped to Cuba."

That voice. I know that voice.

"Just like we planned."

"Excellent. Dante will be pleased."

My breathing stills. No. I recognize both those voices, but it can't be. They were my friends. Why would they do this to me? Who was Dante? And where was Braxton?

Please, Braxton. Find me. I send up a silent plea, praying that he's close, and then the metal doors open and my worst fear comes to life.

FOUR

BRAXTON

"**S**HOULD WE CHECK the port?" Antonio paces in front of my desk.

I called a meeting back in my office for the three men I trust in this famiglia the most. Gio has yet to show up, but I'll take that up with him later. I'm assuming he's out tracking down more leads on Klara's whereabouts.

"My cousin's not stupid. He never planned to send her to Cuba in a fucking shipping container. He knows what Klara means to me. He'd never take eyes off her."

"What does she mean to you, Boss?" Alessandro questions, taking a seat across from me.

I glance down at the glass in my fist, watching the way the liquid swirls with a flick of my wrist. I know the answer I should give as the Don of the mafia. Then there's the answer I want to give. The De Luca family started this famiglia. My great grandfather was the first Don, my grandfather taking over after him, then my father, before the title passed down to me. The title is in my blood, it's what I was groomed for since birth so the answer should be fucking easy. Nothing. She means nothing to me. Say it, De Luca. 'She means nothing to me.' But fuck if nothing comes out when I open my mouth to say those words, because it's the furthest thing from the truth.

I never knew how much was missing in my life until Klara Blouin and that fucking red dress.

If I'm going to do what I'm about to then I need these men with me. There was supposed to be no secrets within the famiglia. They may look at me differently after this but I was still their Don and unless they wanted to be buried six feet under they will still carry out my orders.

"How long have we known each other, Alessandro?"

He shrugs, leaning back in his chair, hooking an ankle over his knee. "Since we were teenagers."

"Do you like being in this famiglia?"

"Braxton…" Antonio cautions, but I hold up a finger, needing to hear Alessandro's answer.

"It's the only family I know, Boss."

I nod and take a sip from the bourbon. "When I'm gone, the title will pass to you."

"Boss?" he questions, sitting up straighter in his seat and glancing between me and Antonio.

"You're my Capo. My second-in-command. No one else I trust more in this famiglia than you, Alessandro."

"Shouldn't that honor go to your first-born son?"

"There will be no son," I reply, finishing my drink and getting up to pour another. "I'll be trading myself for the girl."

"Boss?"

"The fuck?"

They both say in unison.

"Dante has always been a jealous son of a bitch. Always wanting what doesn't belong to him, what he can't have. He wants to take me down, destroy the De Luca name, and at the expense of Klara's life." I turn around, my back toward my two best friends and confidants. "I will not allow that to happen. I'll wager with him. My life for hers."

Antonio sighs from his position across the room. "He gets what he wants and you get to save her life."

"Si. But I'll take him down with me. Klara is not safe in this world if he still breathes. Alessandro will be the new Don."

The room is silent, the only sound the liquid pouring into the glass in my hand.

"Should we tell Gio?" Alessandro asks.

I shake my head, still refusing to turn around and face them, not wanting to see the disappointment in their gaze. When did I become such a pussy? "No, the less who know of this plan the better."

"She really worth all this? To give your life for?" Antonio asks, closer now.

"She's worth so much more."

Shuffling sounds behind me, a hand clasps each of my shoulders and then my office door opens and shuts allowing me to breathe a little easier without an audience to my demise.

I let out a heavy breath, taking a seat behind the desk again and pick up the phone to make the call that will change everything. The call that will lead to my death.

"I'm not giving myself up that easy, Cousin." His voice sends my blood boiling, my hands clenching and unclenching in fists, wishing it was his neck I was squeezing the life from.

"You feel like gambling, Dante?"

"What are the stakes?"

My fucking cousin. Never could resist a good wager. Money or death, he was addicted to both.

"My life for the girl. You get to be at the top for once."

"As tempting as that sounds, you're a little too late, Cuz. Made a pretty penny on that piece of ass. Can see why she caught your attention."

"Dante, I swear to all things holy I'll rip your fucking throat out." I seethe.

"You were always all bark and no bite, De Luca."

Click.

***

(Klara)

"You sonofabitch! You lied to him!" I try twisting in my restraints but the rope burns against the sensitive flesh of my wrists. The muscles in my arms burn from being strung up like a cow at a butcher.

"Lie is such an ugly word, Klara." He taps his chin with a finger. "I prefer motivate."

"He'll kill you."

A strong fist wraps around my hair, yanking my head back and I yelp from the pain. "Si, but he'll have to find me first." He trails a finger around the curve of my breast and I visibly shudder in disgust. "You see, I have someone on the inside. Someone who reports to me whenever De Luca gets too close. Someone who

150

can take him out at any moment. So, his threats… mean nothing to me."

Dante's fingers curl under the neckline of my thin tank top and pull until the material rips down the middle, leaving me completely naked from the waist up. My sleep shorts are the next to go, joining my tank top in a pile on the floor. His hand covering my mouth to keep my screams from being heard.

"But I'm not going to kill him just yet. I want him to come for you. I want to see him break when he realizes I've had my way with you. I want the last thing he sees before he dies to be my cum decorating this lush body of yours. I want him to know, without a doubt, that my hands were the last you felt before you died alongside him. I want him to suffer, and only then will I put him out of misery."

The sound of a zipper being undone sounds behind me seconds before I feel Dante press into me. My hot tears mix with my snot as they run down my face while Dante takes from me, while his hand presses over my mouth, no doubt leaving bruises. For the first time since I was ripped from my bed in the middle of the night, I pray that Braxton doesn't find me. I pray he never sees me like this. Degraded. Used.

I shut my eyes against the sound of Dante grunting behind me and try to will myself back to the last time Braxton and I were together… happy. He fought against our growing relationship for reasons I couldn't understand then, but do now. I saw what I now recognize as a war going on inside him every time his eyes would meet mine. That need to push me away to protect me, but at the same time wanting to pull me closer. I noticed the way his gaze would soften whenever he would look at me when he thought I wasn't looking. I always thought he never paid me much attention while he was working from home, but I was wrong.

"Come here, Mia Bella," Braxton says lifting a blanket from the side of the couch with one hand, and patting the seat next to him with the other.

I bite the corner of my lip not really sure I'm capable of sitting down right now. If I sit then I can't keep pacing and if I can't keep pacing then my thoughts are going to spiral and I need the outlet that pacing allows me to have.

"Klara." Braxton's voice is firm and when I look over at him I know that he's not going to let me off the hook easy.

Reluctantly, I take the seat next to him, curling my legs under me and leaning into his side. Braxton covers us with the blanket and it's at that point that I notice it feels exactly like the gravity blanket I have back at my apartment, but it looks nothing like it. This one is nicer. He settles his arm around my shoulders and pulls me into him more so my head is resting on his chest.

"Talk to me. Why are you pacing a strip in my flooring?"

"They want me to give a speech at graduation next week," I sigh.

"That's great, Mia Bella."

"No," I interrupt his praise. "I mean, yes, it is, but not for me." I sit up slightly so that I can see his face. "Do you know how many people come to these things? Hundreds. Which means I have to stand in front of hundreds of people... all looking at me... and talk." I swallow hard. "I can't do it."

152

"Klara," he whispers, tucking a strand of hair behind my ear. "You can do anything you set your mind to. You are stronger than this anxiety, but if it'll help Alessandro, Gio, and I will be there."

"Braxton, you don't hav --"

"Will it help you deliver your speech if we were there?"

It would. Just knowing that there's someone out in the sea of people who are there for me, other than Adrienne, to cheer me on, who I can look to when it becomes too overwhelming will help significantly. And that's exactly what I tell him.

"Consider it done," Braxton says, placing a soft kiss on my lips then tucking me back into his side and scrolling through Netflix until he comes across my latest show obsession and pressing play.

I think that was the night I realized that falling in love with Braxton De Luca was a real possibility. Now, not only was it just a possibility but a reality because right before I found him in his office, I was ready to tell him that I didn't care what he did for a living, that as long as I got him I could learn to someday be okay with not knowing.

Dante's groan pulls me back to reality and I feel him slide out, hot cum dripping all over my ass before the unmistakable sound of a belt being done up reaches my ears and then a door opens and closes before the lights are shut off.

Darkness.

So, this is what hell looks like.

Footsteps draw near from one of the corners of the room, stopping in front of me but with the lights off I can only just make out the shape of a person. A finger rakes down the side of my face and I flinch away from it.

"I told you not to get involved with him, but you just wouldn't listen. You brought this upon yourself, Klara."

"How could you? You were supposed to be my friend," I sob.

"And you should've listened when I told you to stay away from the De Luca family," Rick snarls.

Tears are flowing freely down my cheeks now as Rick's footsteps fade away in the distance.

***

(Braxton)

I sit at the kitchen counter watching my mother chop vegetables for the beef stew and try not to feel like I'm five years old again while she lectures me about my stupidity when it comes to hurting Klara.

"I'll tell you this though. You're an idiot for letting her go." She shakes her head. "You don't cheat on a woman like her. You hold on tight and don't ever let go. And you pray that you're good enough." She stops chopping and glances up at me pointing the knife in my direction, "but when that girl loves you, you'll know. She'll go out of her way to make you happy. She'll sacrifice for you, and she'll love you like no one ever has before."

"Ma, you sound like you've known her her whole life," I say, taking another drink

"No honey. I just know how to read people."

"Boss, we have a problem," Alessandro announces, walking into my kitchen. He stops when he sees my Ma standing across from me, the counter separating us and the tip of her knife pointed directly at me. One eyebrow raised and a half smirk forming on his lips. Yeah, yeah laugh it up asshole. At thirty-three I'm still getting lectures from my mother.

"Well, don't just stand there, Alessandro," my mother admonishes. "Come. Sit. Dinner will be done shortly."

She waddles over to the pot and throws in the rest of the chopped vegetables. My eyes narrowing at the fact that she's favoring one foot more than the other. I hope her diabetic nerve pain isn't acting up again. We finally got a handle on it with the new medication and she seemed to be doing fine. I mentally shake the thought away. I can't lose both of the important women in my life.

Alessandro looks to me in a silent plea for us to talk somewhere else. "Let's talk in my office," I tell him, walking around the counter to place a kiss on my mother's head. "I'll be back to set the table."

The fact that she doesn't argue, just smiles and pats my arm, is enough to have me worry. She hasn't been her usual self since she got back from her trip to Italy years ago, and I wonder if the extend trip and long flight weakened her already low immune system. I make a mental note to call her doctor in the morning while Alessandro follows me into the office and closes the door behind us.

When I'm sitting down, he hands me a file folder with two pictures inside. One is of a man outside of my cousin's club. His hand firmly clasps in Dante's with Dante's other hand on his shoulder. The second picture is of the same man, only this time he's smiling at the woman next to him while she takes a selfie of the two of them.

Klara.

"Who is this?"

"His name is Richard Belan. Apparently, he and Klara have been friends for almost as long as she's lived here."

I look at the first picture again, studying the way he's interacting with my cousin. They don't look like two people who've just met. They look like they've known each other for years. Alessandro shifts in his seat, sensing my questions and tips his chin toward the picture of Richard and my cousin in my hand.

"Word on the street is that your uncle and Mr. Belan did business together years ago. That's how Dante and Richard met."

"You think this Richard had anything to do with Klara's kidnapping?"

He holds my stare, his eyes never wavering. "Had one of the cops on our payroll talk to the roommate, she said the only other person with access to the apartment is Richard. The guy lives on the floor below them, that's how they met."

I go back to studying the pictures again. Taking in everything Alessandro just told me and hoping like hell that this is the break we need to get closer to finding and bringing Klara home. "Where's he now?" My voice comes out smooth... controlled, the opposite of everything I feel raging within me.

"One of the soldiers just brought him in. He's in the basement."

"Good." I stand up, doing up the two buttons on my suit jacket. "You and Gio get started. I'll join you in a bit."

"Uh," Alessandro clears his throat, looking everywhere but at me.

"What is it, Alex?"

"Gio, Boss. Nobody's heard from him since we dumped that body."

Taking a deep breath, I will myself to stay calm. It's not like Giovanni to do a disappearing act, and he better have a good explanation for it since we're in the middle of a war with my fucking cousin. I'm already antsy, and this isn't helping. With a hand on the doorknob, I turn slightly to look over my shoulder.

"Have Richard brought to the aquarium. I'm thinking a deep dive might be the thing he needs to talk."

FIVE

"**T**AKE THESE THINGS** off. Who are you? Where I am?"

It takes me a minute to remember that the man swinging in front of me, bound by his wrists over the salt-water pool, is in business with my cousin. He looks nothing like the goons Dante employs. He looks more like a soccer player or like he belongs on an ad for a clothing company than a guy who should be doing business with my family.

The monster prowling on the inside wants me to drop him in the water and let the marine life take care of him for putting a hand on Klara. And I'll give it that, but not now. I want to have some fun first and those pictures of him with his arm around Klara and shaking hands with my cousin gives me the motivation I need for what comes next.

"I'm the person your nightmares are based on." I snicker.

His body stills, hands gripping the metal chains around his wrists. "De Luca. Should've known," he mumbles more to himself than for my benefit.

"Ah, so you know who I am." My finger twitches over the button that will send him plummeting through the frigid water.

"It was only a matter of time before you connected the dots and came after me. Torture me all you want, De Luca. You'll never find her."

Glancing down at the tank and making sure nothing is in the way—yet—I press the red button and watch as the line gives, and his body slowly disappears between the glassiness of the surface only for a moment before he's reeled back up again, shivering and coughing up water. His blindfold falling to gather around his neck.

"You underestimate my abilities." I smirk when he starts struggling against his binds which only causes him to swing back and forth.

"Dante's always one step ahead of you, you fuck. He already knows your plans."

And just like that he confirms what I've been speculating about the last twenty-four hours, that there's a traitor within my famiglia. One who was sent by Dante before I took over as Don to keep an eye on me. I have my suspicions, but they're best kept to myself until I know the truth.

"That may be. If he's always one step ahead then are you saying it's no coincidence that you're hanging by your wrists suspended over a pool filled with various marine life that could kill you?"

Richard looks down at the tank beneath his feet, when he glances back up at me there's a smirk on his face and I know exactly what he's thinking.

"Jellyfish? Really? They wouldn't kill me."

I scrub a hand down my growing beard and tap a finger on my chin. "True. Their sting will hurt like hell, and you'll most likely pass out. But I did say could, not that they will kill you. Would you like to test out that theory?"

A slow grin spread across my face as I watch him sink below the surface, the middle of the tank suddenly filling with jellyfish of all sizes. Some touching various areas of his body with their tentacles as they swim for the surface. When I think he's close to passing out, I reel him back up. Various areas of his skin turning an angry red.

"Like I said, they won't kill you. For that I have other plans."

Alessandro chooses that moment to wheel in a smaller tank with one inhabitant and places it in front of me before swapping out the syringe in his hand for the remote in mine. Richard's eyes dart between the pufferfish in the tank and the syringe in my hand.

"Who does he have close to me?"

"Fuck, man, I don't know. I wasn't privy to that information."

I tip my chin and Alessandro lowers him back in the water, in the middle of the school of jellyfish. His screams muffled by the water. He reels him back up a few seconds later.

"You're a sick fuck," he heaves, struggling to breathe through the pain of the stings.

"I am." I chuckle, crouching down to watch the fish through the glass. "Did you know that this little thing carries toxins twelve hundred times more lethal than cyanide?" I glance up at the man still pulling on his binds. "I'm not even sure of the right dose, but this should do it." I straighten to my full height, bringing the syringe up to my eye-level and flicking a finger against it. "So, are you willing to talk, or are you ready to swim with the fishes?" I grin at my horrible joke, but also at the way he visibly pales in front of my eyes.

He curses when the line starts moving, bringing him closer to me but still keeping him hovering over the open tank. Alessandro grabs a hold of his arm on the areas the jellyfish haven't stung and holds him still while I aim the syringe in the crook of his elbow.

"Fuck!" he bellows, trying to twist out of the reach of the needle. "Okay. Okay!"

I stop, the needle resting against his skin and look up at him expectantly.

He sighs, knowing it's either this or death. "Dante never sold her. He's been keeping her for himself. His plan is to get you so enraged that you react on a whim...with no security, so that he can kill you both and take over the famiglia."

Alessandro and I share a look before he nods, a silent communication that he'll start looking for the traitor, and there'll be hell to pay for going against the famiglia.

"Ah, what the fuck!"

Richard's outburst and his eyes rounding in horror as he looks down at his arm causes me to glance down, too. Somehow, in the midst of our exchange, I had pushed the needle into his skin, my thumb pressing down and injecting the lethal toxin.

"You might not want to move around too much. I have no idea how fast that shit spreads." I pull back, dumping the syringe and the gloves into a nearby garbage bag.

"You sonuvabitch! You planned that all along," he yells at my retreating back.

I contemplate his accusation as I shrug into my suit jacket. He's right, of course. I never had any plans of letting him walk out of here alive. "Shouldn't've come between me and what's mine."

***

(Klara)

Braxton's face flashes behind my closed lids. I would give anything to see his face again, to feel the security of his strong arms wrap around me, his lips brushing a soft kiss against my forehead. To hear him say Mia Bella, My beautiful, again. I would give anything to hear him telling me he was no good for me even while pulling me in and holding me tightly against his body. His voice saying one thing but his body saying another.

It wasn't supposed to be like this.

Dante grunts, finishing all over my stomach. Silent sobs rack my body as I grabble for the blanket at the side of the dirty mattress and gingerly pull it over my bruised body. I wasn't allowed to shower, wasn't allowed to wear what little scraps of clothes I had. Dante kept true to his word of wanting to make sure Braxton broke when he eventually saw me. He made sure to remind me that, that time was coming soon and as soon as he had his cousin right where he wanted him he was going to make him watch as he used Braxton's precious blades to carve up my body until it bled dry, and only then would he end Braxton's life.

Dante made sure I looked into his eyes every single time he told me in excruciating detail how he was going to kill me, and then Braxton. He made sure to emphasize that I was only in this hell because Braxton couldn't keep his hands off me, because I became more to the Don of the mafia than I was supposed to be.

Oh yeah, Dante let that little fact slip. That Braxton was in fact head of the Italian mafia, and he made no qualms about the fact that he was insanely jealous of Brax. That the reason behind all of this was because Dante wanted the title of Don and the power that title held.

Strangled cries sounded from the section of room next to mine and I huddled further into my blanket. Sometime during the night, I was brought to this new place. From the sounds I hear at all hours of the day and night, I assume this is where Dante brings the girls he sells into the sex trade. The men have strict orders to not touch me though, unless they want to meet a bloody fate. I was to be used solely for Dante's personal enjoyment.

When did my life become so fucked up? When did I go from falling in love with a man who believes he doesn't deserve to smile, to being used as a pawn in some fucked up game of cat and mouse that was born out of jealousy?

The man I love is the head of one of the biggest crime families in Canada, and one of my best friends sold me out to his cousin. I cover my ears with my hands, shutting my eyes closed against the onslaught of fresh tears in an attempt to block out the sounds of hell, and I do something I vowed to never do again for as long as I lived.

I pray.

I pray not that I make it out of this hellhole, but that a bomb gets dropped on this building, killing me and everyone inside. I pray that the men who hold us here get ripped apart by something more sinister than them. I pray that Braxton gets his hands on Dante, and I pray that he makes the sonofabitch bleed. I pray that he pries finger after finger from his hands, toe after toe from his feet, tooth after tooth from his fucking jaw. I pray that Braxton doesn't let up until Dante is nothing but a pile of broken pieces on the floor because that... that is how Dante has made me feel.

Like trash. Like broken pieces littered on the floor waiting for someone to come along and put them back together.

Who am I kidding. While that vision is incredibly appealing right now, I know that despite the years of trauma these girls will go through if we ever make it out of here alive, if they're strong enough to make it through this hell then they'll be strong enough to survive afterward. And I pray they do. Because there is no bigger fuck you than these girls taking back what was wrongfully taken from them and not allowing these monsters another second to occupy their thoughts.

As I curl into myself I know I'd give anything to see those dark, haunted eyes trained on me again.

***

(Braxton)

"Everything ready?" I ask, rolling up the sleeves of my dress shirt while getting into the back seat of the SUV. Alessandro pockets his phone next to me as Pete, my driver, gets in and starts the vehicle.

"No disrespect, Boss, but you sure this is how you want this to play out?"

I look out my window as we pass by building after building, my elbow propped on the door, absently running my thumb along my bottom lip. Klara loved when I did it, it never failed to draw her gaze to my lips… causing her to bite the corner of her own. I'll never forget the heated look in her eyes when she'd slowly drag those pale blue eyes up my body. It was a look I'd kill to see again.

"Just make sure Antonio and Gio are there."

Alessandro reaches back into his pocket to retrieve his phone and make a couple calls while I settle back against the leather of the backseat and not for the first time, pray that I find my girl.

SIX

Klara

"**THE STUPID SONUVABITCH** got himself killed tonight."

"Did he talk?"

"Don't know. Wasn't there, but knowing Rick it probably didn't take De Luca very much to get anything out of him."

I'm struggling to stay conscious but I can feel my mind wanting to shut down, to live inside my dreams where it's lighter, but I can't let it. Not now. Not when it sounds like Braxton is so close to finding me.

"De Luca called a meeting," the first voice says.

"You think he suspects anything?"

"Don't know. Going to find out."

"Good. Stall him. Need another few days before I'm ready to take over."

There's silence except for the sound of feet moving further and further away, then my mind takes over, and darkness clouds my vision.

***

(Braxton)

"What are we doing here, Boss?" Gio asks, as we around the front of the SUV outside the darkened building.

It took me longer than I cared to admit to find where my cousin has been holed up, but I should've known to look here first. Dante wasn't very smart, he kept recycling buildings for his various activities. His name always attached to the paperwork.

I turn over the cigar in my hand watching it roll between my fingers while Alessandro goes around and collects the cell phones of every man here. It wasn't something I ever required of my men before, but tonight was different. Klara was just on the other side of the brick wall and I wasn't taking any chances of something or someone coming between me and having her back in my arms. And one of these men behind me had betrayed this famiglia. He would not live to see the end of it all.

"We're going to have a little fun," I say out the corner of my mouth while I light up.

Alessandro balls up the bag, stowing it in the trunk of one of the vehicles before coming to stand at my right side, tipping his chin in a slight nod that everything was set. I never once had to question his loyalty, even now with a traitor standing amongst us. Maybe that was because I've known him for half my life, maybe that was because he never once gave me pause to doubt him or his loyalty, but whatever it was, I'm glad for it.

A blacked-out van pulls up alongside our SUV's, several men in uniform filing out the back at the same time an ambulance pulls in behind them. I don't know what was going to go down tonight, but it never hurt to be prepared, and being the head of one of the biggest crime families in the country afford me certain…luxuries. Like having the SWAT team, and any emergency vehicle at my disposal whenever and wherever I needed. I scratched their backs from time to time and they scratch mine.

"You sure you want to involve the RCMP in this?" Antonio asks to my left, keeping his eyes trained on the newly arrived officers.

"Don't know what to expect in there. Need all the man power I can get."

"We could've handled it ourselves, Boss," Gio says next to Antonio.

I look over at the men who are supposed to have my back through whatever shit life dealt us. One of them still does, the other is about to meet a bloody fate. I don't take too well to betrayal. I stand back and listen while the officer in charge gives the rundown of how we'll be breaching the building. I'm not used to taking a back seat in these situations, in fact, I outright despise it, but it was either this or risk killing any women Dante has tied up in there. I may have been willing to take a chance on people's lives, but not innocent women, and certainly not Klara's.

When everyone moves to get into position, I put out my cigar, turning to Alessandro. "Once Klara and the women are free make sure nobody is around. I want him to myself."

He nods, moving to get into position with everyone else, and then all hell breaks loose.

SEVEN

Klara

THE SOUND OF rapid gunfire rouses me, I'd like to say from a deep sleep, but that would be a crock of shit, I wish my mind would've shut off but alas no dice.

I struggle to sit up then bring my knees up to my chest once I'm sitting somewhat steady on the mattress. My muscles ache from being subject to this mattress that is nothing but broken springs and worn fabric, and from the hours of torture I've had to endure since being brought here. The men here may have been ordered to not touch me, sexually, but that didn't mean they couldn't use me as their own personal punching bag. I got a few good hits in at first before I realized that they wanted me to fight back, they fed off of it, and the more I fought the harder they hit.

With shaky arms, I push myself to my knees ready to crawl to the curtain and make a run for it if the coast was clear. No restraints were a result of all the beatings, they figured if they beat me down enough then there was no reason to restrain me because surely I would be weak enough to not contemplate running. Just wait until I get my hands on them. I'll show those fuckers weak.

But just as I place my palms on the cold ground to get ready to crawl, my curtain is pushed open and I freeze, bile raising up the back of my throat. I don't look up as the air around me becomes thicker making it harder to breathe.

No, dammit. This was supposed to be my chance for escape.

Black leather dress shoes appear in my vision and I swallow past the lump in my throat. If I'm dreaming, this is the worst nightmare ever. And then dark eyes appear in front of me. Dark hair, full lips, a five o'clock shadow that's way past five o'clock, a strong jaw as it ticks with his anger.

"Klara." That voice. My name coming from those lips is enough for whatever strength I had left to flee and I shatter into a million pieces right here on this cold cement floor, naked and dirty on my knees in front of Braxton.

"I've got you, Mia Bella." His voice breaks as he pulls me onto his lap, wrapping those strong arms around me and pulling me further into him. A warm blanket gets draped over my body and Braxton murmurs a thank you to whoever delivered it before resting his chin on the top of my head, my body shaking from the never-ending onslaught of cries and screams emanating from a part of me I locked away during this whole ordeal.

***

(Braxton)

"It's time," Alessandro informs me, but I'm not ready to let Klara out of my sight yet. Maybe I'll never be ready.

I know I'll never forget the sight of her when I opened that curtain. All of Dante's men had been taken out, my cousin nowhere to be found, and we were going from curtain to curtain discovering girls of all ages, some younger than eighteen, bruised and broken, cowering in the corner and crying because they thought we were just more of the monsters they've had to deal with for god knows how long.

The beast inside me is sitting on his haunches expectantly at the door of his cage, his teeth bared in a snarl because he knows I'm about to let him out to play and he's all too eager after witnessing what my cousin had going on in this building, and finding Klara the way we had. It pisses me off that Dante got away, but I won't rest until I have his head in my hands and my concrete floor is stained red with his blood. His running only adds to further ignite the anger coursing through my veins.

I stand up with Klara in my arms. My heart swells with the way she attempts to burrow further into me, like no matter how hard she tries she'll never get closer. She could burrow her way under my skin for all I care and I would let her stay there, surrounded by my warmth, in the protection only I can provide her.

"Antonio." I motion for him to follow me out to the ambulance where I deposit Klara, unwillingly, onto the bed.

"Stay with her. Don't let her out of your sight until I get back, you hear me?" I grab the collar of his shirt, pulling him right into me until our noses are just inches apart.

"Got it."

I move to walk away but Klara's grip on my hand tightens, her eyes rounding in fear.

"Gio?" Her voice is small, panicked.

I give her the most reassuring smile I can manage right now, loving the way she leans her face into my palm when I cup her cheek. "I know, Klara. I'm going to end this, and then you and me... we'll go home."

I look back to Antonio. His jaw ticks with the realization of what her words meant, and then reluctantly I turn and go in search of where Alessandro has been holding the man who stabbed in me the back.

***

The sonofabitch grins. "Looks like you've just seen a ghost, Boss." He snickers even with blood running down his face and Alessandro's gun trained on him. One nod from me and his brains will be splatters across the walls.

"You betray me? Betray this family?!" I bellow, my voice echoing against the walls.

"Was never a part of your fucking family," he snarls, his top lip raising, exposing a gap where his tooth should've been.

"Never part of this fucking family," I repeat, running a thumb over my bottom lip, glancing over his shoulder. "You hear this fucking shit, Alex?"

He nods. "Sure did, Boss."

I glare at Gio. "Trusted you with my life. With Klara's life. Let you sit at my Ma's table, eat dinner with us. Took you into my confidence and this... this is how you show your respect, by helping my cousin sell Klara into the sex trade!" I barely have a grip on my anger. If I were just five minutes later, I may have never found Klara. May have never gotten her back.

"You never deserved the title of Don. You're weak. Putting the life of one girl before the famiglia," Gio spits.

The warehouse door swings open, blinding light illuminating the figure entering. If I thought I barely had a handle on my anger before, I fucking lose it now as the door closes revealing Klara in nothing but my black button up dress shirt and a pair of beaten up boots.

"Klara, thought I told you to stay with Antonio," I seethe, hating the fact that she's in the same room as the person who betrayed me, who stole her from under my nose. I was as infuriated at him as I was myself.

"And I told you I didn't need a babysitter!" she bites back, and I have to try to hold back a smirk. My girl's fucking beautiful when that fire lights behind her eyes.

"Mia Bella, you don't need to see this."

She scowls, a line forming between her perfectly sculptured eyebrows. "I know it makes you uncomfortable having me here, seeing this part of your life, but I do, in fact, need this. I need to see him pay for what he did with my own two eyes. I need to be able to close my eyes without seeing his face. I need to be able to sleep at night. I need..." her voice breaks and it takes every bit of strength I have left to not pull her into my arms.

Every fiber of my being is screaming at me to protect her, to shield her against what is about go down in this room, but I've seen that look in her eyes before. That steely determination, the look of someone who's been through hell and somehow clawed their way up the other side, someone who fought their way back from the brink of death. Someone who's one step closer to shutting the blinds on their heart and encasing themselves in darkness. Fucking fuck!

Alessandro shifts on the other side of the room behind Gio and I know he's thinking the same thing. He doesn't like her being here anymore than I do because he wants to protect her from this life as much as me.

"Braxton." Klara places a hand on my arm, earning her my glare but she doesn't show any fear. A glare that has been known to bring grown men to their knees and beg forgiveness, and this woman doesn't even fucking flinch. "Please... I need this. Give me this."

I blow out a breath, the beast inside bearing its teeth in a snarl. There's nothing about this situation that I'm okay with, but I realize now that it's not about me. No matter how much I want to be the Don and tell her—no, demand her—to go back outside and wait with Antonio, no matter how much I want to push her behind me and protect her with my life, to shield her from the ugly side of this life, it's. Not. About. Me.

It's about her and the nightmare she had to live from the second those bastards got their hands on her, to when my cousin marked her, to being forced to display her body to those... bile raises up my throat thinking about the hell my girl had to live through when I couldn't save her fast enough. The truth is, she's

174

already seen the ugly side of this life. She's already lived it and survived it.

My eyes survey the scene around me. So this… this isn't by far the ugliest, and if this is what she needs to feel safe again then I'll bring every single one of the sick fucks back from death and drag them in here by the skin of their teeth, and string them up for her to do with as she pleases. If this is what's going to help her heal then she can fucking have it, and I'll give it to her willingly.

I nod, shooting a warning glare at Alessandro when he starts to protest, and offer Klara the option of the pair of matching blades I'm always carrying, or the set of 24k Gold Desert Eagles that I never leave home without. The same pair of guns my father gave me the day I became a man. The day I had my first taste of blood, of death.

She surprises the fuck out of me by choosing the blades, her hand hovering over the shiny metal of the handles.

"Klara, you don't need to do this." I try again to change her mind. Murder is not an easy path to come back from.

She blows out a breath, determination in her eyes when her fingers curl around the handles. "I know, but I have to."

My palm wraps around one of the desert eagles, while my other hand reaches back and replaces the second one in its holster at my side.

"This is a conversation for the men, little girl," Gio snarls, not knowing that he just sealed his fate at the hands of my girl. "Run along now. This is no place for you."

It's quick, but I don't miss the way her hand veers to the side and then quickly cuts back, slicing through the fabric and skin of his chest. I grin when Gio falls to his knees, clutching his gaping wound in one arm, and doubles over. His breath heavy.

Klara uses the toe of her boot to kick him so he's lying on his back, his wound exposed as she stands over him, careful not to let him see under the shirt. I growl in warning, my hand tightening around the eagle in my palm. One wrong move and I'll put the fucker down myself.

I wince when her foot comes up and settles over his open wound, the flexing of the muscles in her leg and Gio's agonizing screams are the only signs of her putting pressure on the fresh cut.

"You tried to push me off the CN Tower that day on the EdgeWalk, didn't you?"

What the fuck?

I look over at Alessandro, the knuckles of his hands are turning white as he clenches his fists tighter at that new revelation.

Gio laughs despite the obvious pain he's in. "Yeah, if it wasn't for that stupid rope they had us tied to, you would've gone over, too. Saved me a shit load of trouble. You were so ready to trust me, and all I did was bring you junk food and sit through a few episodes of that horrid tv show." He groans with the increased pressure she puts on his wound. "Tell me, little girl, do you spread your legs so easily for any man who shows you the slightest bit of attention?"

I see it the second it happens, the little bit of life that was left in her eyes fades. My girl shuts down right in front of me with her booted foot grinding down on

Gio's wound, and the other blade hovering a few feet in the air over his groin. Any humanity that was left inside of her dies when her fingers uncurl, sending the blade in a free fall. I feel like howling right along with Gio when the sharp edges connect with its target.

Klara smirks, watching over her shoulder as blood pours from the wound around the floor beneath him. Then she shrugs, making sure he's looking directly at her when she leans down and lowers her voice. "You didn't need them anyway. It's not like you were a real man. Consider it payback."

She straightens up, handing the other knife to Alessandro before turning around and walking to stand in front of me. Klara places her hands, palms down on my chest and leans up to place a kiss on my lips. "Make it hurt, baby. I'll be waiting outside."

Moonlight streams in as she yanks open the warehouse door and disappears into the night.

EIGHT

Klara

I DON'T KNOW what possessed me to walk through that door and do what I just did. I had no desire to see Gio, Rick, or Dante ever again, but I also had this overwhelming knowledge that if I didn't walk in there and confront my demons head on then I wouldn't be able to start the healing process, and if I ever wanted to put the last week behind me and have a chance of a future with Braxton then I needed to heal. And I had to make sure those bastards paid with their life.

Antonio is pacing a line in the pavement as I make my way back toward the ambulance where I left him. His head shoots up at the sound of my approaching footsteps.

"You're going to get me killed," he accuses, pointing a finger in my direction. His mouth opens like he wants to say more but shuts at the expression on my face. He opens his arms, his fingers bending in a 'come here' gesture and I rush into them, not realizing I'm crying until I feel the wetness on his shirt under my cheek. "I'm sorry, baby girl. We should've gotten here sooner."

"I'm just glad you guys came at all," I manage between hiccups. "I was beginning to think…" I shut my eyes against the ambush of memories, and the thoughts that ran through my head the past week.

"I know what you were thinking, baby girl, and I don't want you to ever entertain that thought. Braxton… he will come for you. No matter where you are, he'll come for you. There's no mountain high enough, no ocean wide enough that he will not fight to make sure you're back in his arms." His arms tighten around my heaving body. "Alessandro and I… we'll be right there with him."

"But why though, Antonio? You barely know me." My voice comes out muffled against his shirt.

"Know all I need to. Never seen Braxton the way he was this week. He was ready to trade himself for you, baby girl. Ready to give up all he's known for you… ready to die for you."

My head rises and falls with the rhythm of his breathing. Antonio takes in a deep breath, hands on my shoulders, and gently pushes me away so he can get a better look at my face. "Klara, Braxton isn't an easy man to love. He wants you to be his, but after this week he'll either push you further away, or he'll pull you close and be even more of a possessive, arrogant bastard. If he pushes you away, you fight for him, yeah? You don't give up on him."

"And if he pulls me in?"

Antonio grins. "You give him hell. He'll want eyes on you all the time, he won't be able to focus until he knows where you are. Give him that for the first bit, but don't let the bastard walk over you. He'll loosen up when he realizes you're not going anywhere."

I cross my arms under my chest. "I'm not going anywhere, Antonio. I still want him as much as I did two years ago. He may have forgotten about me, but I never... not once... forgot about him."

"He never forgot about you, Klara. Why do you think we're here?"

I shrug. "Because Dante sent him my picture and he felt guilty? I honestly don't know anymore."

"His ex did a number on him when she left like she did, but Braxton... he loves you. Dante realized Braxton's feelings for you before Braxton did himself. He'll never be able to live with himself if anything happened to you."

"Braxton doesn't love me. He pushed me away all those years ago."

"Si, but I do love you, Mia Bella. It just took me a long time to realize it."

I freeze at the sound of his voice. Antonio's grin grows into a full smile that I want to slap off his face. "You knew he was there?"

He nods, leaning back against the side of the ambulance, a smug look on his face. I narrow my eyes at him, letting him know that he'll be paying for that later, and then turn around to face my fate.

"It took two years and me getting kidnapped for you to realize that you love me?"

I don't know why my bitch mode is activated right now. This man just saved me from hell, the least I could do was thank him and be grateful.

Slowly, deliberately, he runs a thumb over his bottom lip. A slow half grin pulling at the corner of those lips. "I'm a slow learner."

"More like ancient," I mumble under my breath.

Braxton stalks toward me. I notice, not for the first time, how I love the way his muscles move under his shirt. Then he's standing right in front of me, his hands in my hair, his breath on my face.

"Did you just sass me, Mia Bella?"

I close my eyes, leaning into his touch, trying to soak up as much of his heat as humanly possible. "Mmhm." I hum, the events of the past week suddenly catching up to my body and my adrenaline of the last couple hours slowly dwindling away. We stand in the middle of the chaos in the parking lot, Braxton's arms folded around me, my fingers clutching the fabric of the shirt at his back as my eyes slowly droop closed.

Before I know it, I'm cradled in his arms, my head against his chest and my arms securely around his neck. Safely in Braxton's arms, sleep comes fast.

NINE

ALESSANDRO

THE WOMAN BURIED against my chest is small, barely fitting in the fold of my arms. She can't be much older than eighteen. She's all skin and bone, her face sunken. What I'm assuming was once a shiny halo of chocolate brown hair is now dull and lifeless.

I don't want to give her up. Something in me is pleading for us to keep her, to encase her in a protective bubble so nothing else can hurt her ever again. I know I can't offer her the medical attention she needs though, and after watching what Braxton went through with Klara, I know without a doubt that this life is no place for a woman. Not one who has the potential to make me care more than I'd like.

Reluctantly, I place her in the waiting ambulance. Another perk of having the entire city on the boss's payroll is having all the emergency response vehicles at your beck and call with no questions asked, but when she grips my hand in hers I can't bring myself to let go.

Her emerald eyes plead with me to not let go. I'm captivated by them, by the haunted look in their depths, by the flecks of gold swirling in them.

"Are you coming with us?" one of the paramedics asks hesitantly.

Closing my eyes, I let out a fast breath and slip my hand from hers. Already regretting my decision when I open them and see the tears pooling in her eyes as her hand falls away.

Shaking my head, I try and convey how sorry I am without words and then do the last thing I want and turn my back on her.

I'll forever be haunted by the girl with the emerald eyes.

TEN

Klara

TAKING A DEEP breath, I pull my shoulders back as I look up at the massive house in front of me, realizing for the first time I've been able to take in the front of the house. The other times I was here we drove right into the four-car garage and I only caught glimpses of the outside through the window.

House is putting what sits in front of me mildly. It's huge, like sticks out like a sore thumb in the city huge. I smirk at myself. That was probably his idea when he had it built. I mentally give myself a shake, I'm not here to stare at the gorgeous monstrosity in front of me, but my feet don't move. Thankfully, my best friend must sense my hesitation through some sort of bestie telepathic connection because my phone vibrates in my pocket a second later.

Dri: You got this!

Me: What if he's changed his mind?

Dri: He hasn't. And he'd be an idiot if he has.

When I woke up in the hospital, Dri was the only one there. She spent many nights curled up on those crappy visitor chairs in the hospital room, or wrapped around me when I couldn't stand the sight of her body contorted in weird angles in the chair. It took her awhile to confess to me that it scared the shit out of her when she found out I was missing. It terrified her even more when I later divulged that Rick was behind my kidnapping. I was beyond grateful to hear that she was never touched. I think that had mostly to do with her never being at our apartment and spending nights with Matt. Dri said she couldn't stand to be alone in that apartment after what happened to me. She also made it clear that, that meant in no way were the two of them together. I smirk, knowing that it was only a matter of time before Matt broke down her walls.

Through the last month, Dri barely left my side. She went full mama bear mode on me; making sure I was okay, that I ate, that the bruises were healing. She made me talk about what happened in that building, and although I hated reliving it I knew it was a necessary evil in my road to healing. But never, not once, did Braxton come see me.

I haven't seen Braxton in almost a month, since the day he rode in the ambulance with me to the hospital. The only communication with him being the random texts in the middle of the night, or care packages sent from his mom delivered by Alessandro. I think they both feel guilty for not knowing Gio had played us all. More so them than me. I mean, he did befriend me and try to gain my confidence in order to kidnap me, but he pretended to be part of their family for years. Worked alongside them. Killed alongside them. That's why I gave Braxton his space, and tried not to take it personally when he never came to see me. Antonio's words replay in my head.

If he pushes you away, you fight for him, yeah? You don't give up on him.

So here I am, standing outside his house, ready to fight for him. It's been thirty days, and I'm tired of waiting. I take an anxious step forward, and another, and another, until I'm staring at the doorbell next to the front door.

Before I can lift a finger to ring it, the front door swings open revealing Braxton's mother standing on the other side, dark as night hair pinned in a neat bun on top her head, her usual apron tied around her middle, one hand on her hip, the other holding the door open.

"It's about time you showed up," she scolds, narrowing her eyes at me as I hesitantly stand on the other side of the door.

"Um—"

"I was expecting you sooner." She cuts me off. "You never fazed me as the type of girl to take any shit, especially from my son. He needs a strong woman." She opens the door wider, motioning for me to come in.

"I, uh…" I take a couple tentative steps forward, not really sure what the right thing to say is, or what to say at all, really. "He never, uh…" I sigh, not getting anywhere with my words. When I look up at his mom, there's a huge smile plastered on her face.

"He's been holed up in that office of his for quite some time." She tips her head to the side indicating the door down the hall. "Maybe you're just the person to entice him out." She pats my arm lovingly, and then retreats back into the kitchen, but not before calling out that dinner will be done shortly.

Well, it's now or never, Klara.

I slowly make my way down the hall. Mentally preparing myself for what I may find on the other side. After all, the last time I was making my way toward one of Braxton's office doors, the scene I walked in on was not one I care to relive. Ever.

I knock, my knuckles rasping against the wood three times before I twist the handle and push my way inside. I was ready for anything, ready to face anything that awaited me when I walked into his office. Anything but the scene in front of me.

Braxton is hunched forward in the seat behind his desk, his elbows on his knees. A glass tumbler of amber liquid dangling from the tips of his fingers. A hand running through his hair, his head bowed, eyes trained on the ground.

He looks... broken, but so was I and I needed him.

"So, that's it? You're just going to run away again? Un-fucking-believable."

"Leave, Klara." His tone is sharp, meant to hurt.

This is exactly what Antonio warned me about. That Braxton would try to push me further away, but I'm not going to let him this time. He never stopped fighting to save me, so I refuse to stop fighting for him.

"No."

"You shouldn't have to see me like this." He tips his head back, taking another gulp of the liquor, but never lifting his eyes from their downward gaze.

"You don't always have to be the strong one, Brax. You're allowed a moment of weakness every now and then, but your done running away when shit gets hard."

His glass goes flying through the air as he shoots up out of his seat. I try not to jump at the sound of the glass shattering, instead choosing to focus on his bare chest heaving, the skin turning red. "I'm the Don, Klara. I'm always supposed to be fucking strong. If I showed even one second of weakness, people around me start dying. You almost died because I was weak."

"No," I argue, walking further into the room, closer to him. "I almost died because your cousin couldn't handle the fact that you're a better head of the family than he ever hoped to be." I round the desk on shaking legs until I'm toe-to-toe with my monster. "Because they were afraid of the amount of power you wield, of what you could do to them." I reach up, linking my hands behind his head and forcing his forehead down to rest against mine. "What happened to me was not your fault, Braxton."

We're quiet for a long time, but the question I've been needing the answer to is eating away at me.

"Why did you tell me? That you're the head of the Mafia?"

"Because the less you knew about me the better. I told you this life wasn't safe, Klara. There'll always be people who think they can take me down and that threat extends to you if you're by my side. I saw my ma live through it my whole life, I was not going to make you do the same. If you died in that building…"

"I didn't die. You saved me."

"What if I'm too late next time?" He tries to hide the crack in his voice, but I heard it. And everything clicks in to place.

He was too late to save his sister, the one other person he loved more in this world and he never forgave himself for it. None of what happened to his sister was his fault, but Braxton carries the weight of the world on his shoulders and it was pointless in telling him that he didn't have to feel guilty for his sister's death. He needed to come to that conclusion himself.

I don't know how to answer his question because he's right. There could be a next time, and that should scare me but it surprisingly doesn't. What scares me is the possibility of going another two years without him. Of not being in his arms twenty, thirty years from now. So, I don't answer him. Instead, I hold onto him tighter.

His hands slide around my waist, gripping the fabric at my lower back and pull me forward crushing me into his chest. He dips his head, burying his nose in the crook of my neck, and I can breathe a little easier because this feels like home. This man feels like my home. A man who wears his darkness like a crown of glory, a man I should be running far away from instead of clinging to.

"Not ever going to let you go again, Mia Bella."

"I don't want you to let go, Braxton."

We stand like this for a while, gripping onto each other, neither one wanting to be the first to let go. Crying together. Grieving for the parts of us that were lost over the last several weeks, well the last few years. And ready to accept that we'll never have to go at life alone again, that we'll always have each other.

Before I'm fully ready to move on, there is one thing I need Braxton to do.

"I need you to erase his hands from my body. Need you to replace his touch with your own," I whisper into his shoulder, and feel the vibration of the growl in his chest.

Braxton takes hold of my hand, leading me out of the office and down the hall. He says something to his mother about being late for dinner before he's pulling me up the stairs and shutting his bedroom door behind us.

***

(Braxton)

"Do you remember your safe word, baby?"

Her lips part slightly and she nods. She looks fucking beautiful with her hands bound above her head with my crimson red silk tie, and the black blindfold covering her eyes, taking up half her face.

"Good. Now, lay still," I command.

"Brax..." Her breaths are getting heavier, the lower my lips skim her torso, down her belly to place kisses at the apex of her thighs.

"Hmm, I can smell your arousal, Klara." I run my nose up her slit, inhaling her scent and causing her to shiver.

"Brax, please," she begs, little mewls leaving her throat as my lips just barely skim where she wants me.

"You want my mouth, baby?"

"Yes," she pants, spreading her legs further for me.

I nip the insides of her thighs and then lean over her, tugging her earlobe between my teeth before whispering, "not yet."

Klara groans and I chuckle, running my tongue over her collar bone and nipping that spot where her shoulder meets her neck. My fingers gentle gliding down the side of her breast, down her ribs, her leg before working their way back up the inside.

She arches into me, a silent plea for me to touch her, to grant her the release she's so desperately craving. But I won't. Not yet.

I'm still getting used to having my girl back in my arms after she was ripped away from me. I need to savor the feel of her skin under my fingers a little while longer to make sure I really do have her back.

I lick up her neck while my fingers continue their assault; running one down her slit, inserting just the tip, only to withdraw again and circle her clit. I repeat the motion over and over again while kissing that sweet spot behind her ear that awards me with a shiver every. Damn. Time. And it doesn't disappoint.

"Dammit," Klara huffs. "I don't want sweet, and I don't want gentle right now, Braxton. I don't want you to make love to me. I need you to fuck me. I need it rough, Brax. I need it violent. I need you…unleashed." Her pleading pale eyes find my dark ones. "Fuck me. Make me scream. Mark my skin. Just please, make me forget," she pants, bucking into my hand when it draws near to her slit again.

I pull back, grip her hips, and flip her onto her stomach. Pulling her up onto all fours and leaning my front into her back, my one hand snakes around to grip her throat, while my other tugs at a nipple.

"You want rough, Mia Bella?" I growl in her ear. "You want violent? You want to unleash the monster, Klara?" I buck my hips, my cock rubbing up the seam of her luscious ass.

She moans, wiggling her ass against me and I groan, my fingers digging into her hip hard enough that

I may have just left finger-shaped bruises on her skin, halting her movements. When she stills, I loosen the grip on her hip and move to palm her pussy.

"Answer me," I hiss at the same time I plunge a finger inside her wet heat.

"Oh, God, yes! I want —"

"Be sure of what you're asking of me, Mia Bella," I warn, adding a second then third finger to the assault, curling them and finding her g-spot.

"Please," she begs. "Make me forget, Braxton. I need you."

Those three little words are enough to make me snap, to give her exactly what she wants, what she's been begging for.

I need you.

I release my grip around her throat, move her ash blonde hair over her shoulder with one of my hands while the other continues its rhythmic thrusts in and out of her pussy.

"Lean forward and place your hands on the headboard. Do not let go, Klara. If you let go, it'll get worse. Understand?"

She nods, doing exactly what I've asked of her.

"Good. What's your safe word?"

"Kitten," she moans, grinding her hips against my hand seeking more friction, but I don't allow her to find it.

"Good girl. Now, open your mouth." Removing my fingers from her pussy, I bring them to her mouth and watch as she licks around them, pulling them in and sucking my fingers clean of her juices. Klara's eyes close on a moan and my cock twitches behind the zipper of my pants. Her hands never once leaving their hold on the headboard.

She releases my fingers from her mouth with a pop. I grip her chin between my thumb and forefinger and crash my mouth down on hers. Tasting her arousal on her tongue. Fuck me, but she tastes incredible. Sweet. I nip at her bottom lip hard enough to cause her to whimper.

"Last time I'm going to ask, little one. Are you sure?"

She gulps, a flash of uncertainty in her eyes, but then it's gone, and she nods.

I move to stand at the foot of the bed, admiring her spread for me. Her plump ass offered up to me do it with as I please. I press a palm to the raging hard on behind my zipper and let out a slow breath.

Klara has allowed me to introduce her to new heights, new toys in the past. Before she was taken from me. But this, this was going to be different. What I let her see before was only a fraction of what I was capable of. I never allowed myself to fully let go with her in the bedroom, but I couldn't deny her now. Not when she looked me in the eyes and begged for it.

Sweet Jesus, she had begged for it. Begged me to get violent. To mark her.

A low growl rumbles up my throat when Klara pushes that ass further into my palms as I run them up and down each cheek.

"Going to mark this beautiful skin, Klara. Going to mark it so good you won't be able to sit for a week without thinking of me."

"Ah," she groans when I sink my teeth into the globe of her ass.

Reaching down next to me, I grip the cool leather in my hand and resume my stance at the foot of the bed. "Remember that safe word, baby," I reiterate again.

"Please, Brax…ah!" she cries out when the leather hits her skin, instantly turning it red. I run a soothing hand over the angry skin, but then my dirty girl begs for more.

Smack!

The leather of the flogger turns more of her skin a supple red.

Smack!

Smack!

Klara moans, the evidence of her arousal running down her inner thighs. My cock jumps and strains against its confines. I'm not ready for it to come out and play yet so it'll just have to wait a little longer before we're balls deep inside her.

Walking over to the far wall, I slide open the wooden drawer and locate the object I'm looking for as well as a bottle of lube. For what I have planned next, we're going to need it.

"Grip that headboard, baby," I rasp, leaning down on my haunches so I'm eye level with the part of her body I'm eager to play with.

Klara hisses when the cold liquid hits the sensitive skin of her ass, then lets out the sexiest moan when I spread the lube around her tight hole.

"You going to give me all of you, Mia Bella?"

She shivers when my breath glides over her skin. "Yes," she sighs.

"Take a deep breath and relax. Let me in, baby."

She instinctively pushes against me when I slide a finger past the tight ring of muscle. Klara immediately exhales when my finger is fully seated in her ass, and as a reward I smooth my palm over her ass cheek.

When she relaxes enough and gets used to one finger, I insert another, and another. My cock jumps at the sight of her tight hole taking three of my fingers, and I bite back a groan.

"Ah, fuck! Brax...I need...I need more."

I grin, withdrawing my fingers. I slick up the toy with lube and add a bit more to her hole. Without warning, I push the head of the dome-shaped toy past the ring of muscle. Klara groans until it's fully seated except for the base.

I crawl up behind her, trailing kisses along her spine as I go. I circle her clit with the hand that wasn't just deep inside her ass and Klara shudders.

"Can't wait anymore, Mia Bella. Going to fuck you hard now," I growl close to her ear, my fingers leaving her clit to undo my belt and unzip my pants. In one fluid motion, I line up the head of my cock at her entrance and thrust in. Klara's head falls back against my shoulder as she screams out.

"Fuck. So tight, baby," I grunt, pumping in slow, languid stokes, giving her a few seconds to get used to my length again. But a few seconds is all I give her before my hand curls around her throat again, forcing her to lean up and back into me slightly.

And then I let her have exactly what she asked me for.

I fuck her. Hard. Never giving her a reprieve.

She mewls causing me to thrust harder. Fuck, it's almost violent now.

"You like that, baby? Your pussy's taking a beating."

"Oh, fuck! Oh, god!"

I chuckle. "No, baby. It's all me. When you come all over my cock, you're going to scream my name and only my name. Understand?"

"Yes! Fuck, yes!" she pants.

I grip her chin between my fingers, forcing her head back to me and devour her mouth at the same time my fingers find her clit, the walls of her pussy clenching around my cock making stars dance behind my closed lids.

"That's it. Come for me, baby. Scream my name."

I slightly change the angle of my hips and thrust. In and out. In and out.

With a butt plug in her tight hole, my cock in her pussy, my fingers against her clit, and my tongue in her mouth, Klara squeezes around me, and then her whole body shudders as her orgasm rushes through her.

"Oh, fuck! Braxton!"

When she starts coming down from her orgasm, I withdraw and replace the butt plug with my cock. Klara stiffens at first when the head of my cock starts pushing past the ring of muscle but relaxes again when my fingers continue rubbing her clit.

Tiny shudders still shake her body from her recent high, but I can't wait. I want this part of her. I need this part of her. I want to see my come drip out of this tight hole.

Klara moans when I push all the way in. My hold around her throat falling away, instead choosing to wrap her long hair around my fist and tug forcing her back to arch even more.

"Whose ass is this?"

"Yours," she groans as I continue my bruising assault. Klara's moans and pants get louder the faster I pump into her tight ass. And then a second orgasm crashes through her as she screams my name.

"Damn right it's mine," I grunt, and follow with my own release.

We collapse in a sweat heap in the middle of the bed, Klara snuggles into me and my arm automatically goes around her to bring her closer. I don't fucking cuddle. Never have. But with her, I'd do damn near just about anything.

ELEVEN

"UM. BRAXTON?" KLARA asks, propped up by an elbow on the bed, watching as I pull on a clean pair of pants. It's been two weeks since the night she showed up in my office and I thank god for that. The light has slowly started coming back in her eyes, and with every passing day she's looking more and more like the Klara I started falling in love with.

"Yeah, babe?"

"Why do you have Victoria tattooed on your ass in a heart?"

I curse, forgetting I even had that damn tattoo. "Klara Victoria Blouin," I say, like that answers her question as to why I got the damn thing.

"You got my middle name tattooed on your ass?"

I run a hand over my face and sigh. "I was drunk. Never did know how to handle my bourbon. It was a spur of the moment decision that Antonio tried to talk me out of, but I may have threatened to cut off a limb." I shrug, turning back to face her. "I don't exactly remember what was threatened."

Klara giggles and it's the sweetest fucking sound I've ever heard.

"I can't believe you have my name tattooed to your ass."

"An ass that now belongs to you, Mia Bella." I grin over at her after I push my arms through a clean dress shirt.

"Damn straight it does."

Klara slips out of bed, the satin sheet sliding down to reveal her very naked body to my view, and I groan wishing like all hell that I could spend the day exploring that body. Especially when she reaches up to fix my tie and her breasts push against my chest.

"You going to be waiting for me when I get home?" I ask, placing kisses along her jaw, at the corner of her mouth.

"You can't get rid of me that easily, De Luca."

***

(Klara)

The doorbell rings while I'm in the middle of preparing Braxton's favorite meal for dinner. His mother may have let it slip that he's sucker for a good homemade mac and cheese with real bacon pieces crumbled throughout. She offered to lend me her recipe but lucky for me, it was my specialty so I already my own ready to go.

Covered in flour and cheese sauce I hurry to get the door since Pete is with Braxton at the office downtown and I haven't seen Alessandro or Antonio all day, not like those two would answer the door even if they were here.

A tall, brunette stands on the other side, her body tightly encased in a black dress. I'm almost afraid that if she breathes, the seams on the dress will give and rip apart.

"Can I help you?" I ask tipping my head to the side.

A smirk forms on her lips as her darks eyes take me in from head to toe. "When did Braxton get a cook? Did mommy dearest finally decide to stop babying him?"

I start to answer but she cuts me off with a wave of her hand so I clamp my mouth shut and raise an eyebrow.

"It doesn't matter. Is Braxton home?"

"And who are you exactly?" I plant myself firmly between her and the entrance way, crossing my arms under my chest.

"I'm Amanda. His ex-fiancée. Well, hopefully soon-to-be fiancée again. Now, run along and tell your boss that I'm here." She shoos me.

My grin grows as I realize that this was the bitch Braxton told me about last night after hours of lovemaking. His ex-fiancée who left him for his cousin right before they were supposed to get married. Who the fuck does that? Okay, I admit it wasn't the greatest conversation to have while lying naked and entangled together, but he felt like he needed to be honest with me about his past. He also told me about the little visit he paid to his cousin's club and his run-in with Amanda. In a way, I'm glad she left him because if she hadn't then he wouldn't be mine and there's no way in hell I'm giving him up without a fight this time. I was all too willing to walk away from him when he pushed me away before, but not this time. I'd happily fight the bitch if she thinks she can waltz back into his life and reclaim her position.

Little frown lines appear on her forehead when she realizes that I'm not moving and have no intention to move. "Why aren't you going to tell him I'm here?" It's almost comical the way she's pouting. Like she hasn't quite grown up from her teenage years.

'Because I doubt my husband would be interested to know that some slut who is just after his money is on his front step." Okay, so Braxton wasn't my husband, and we haven't discussed that topic yet, but she doesn't know that and I'm trying everything in my power to not bitch slap her right now.

"Klara, who's at the door?" Alessandro's heavy footfalls sound behind me. Ah, so they are in the house.

"Nobody important," I call over my shoulder, but then I didn't need to because he's right behind me in the next second.

Amanda's mouth gapes open as she takes in how comfortable I am around Braxton's second-in-command, but she recovers quickly and I'll give her credit for that. "Alex, who is this girl?" she says, motioning toward me.

Alessandro grins, looking down at me and placing a reassuring hand on my shoulder. "Klara is Braxton's wife," he reiterates my earlier claim.

Is it bad that I'm getting a kick out of watching her visibly squirm in her designer heels that are way too high? No? Okay. Just checking.

"Well, can you just tell him that I came by?"

This bitch just doesn't give up. I grip the edge of the door in my hand, slowly pulling it closed but stop when she's barely visible. "Not likely. Braxton will no longer be needing your services."

"He's a dead man if my husband ever gets his hands on him," she yells through the crack, and I laugh, because it's either that or cry at the mention of Dante.

"Not if mine catches him first," I bite back, slamming the door in her face and immediately leaning my back against the painted wood.

"You handled that well, baby girl," Alessandro hands me a glass of wine, bless him, and then retreats back to the living room with me hot on his heels.

After putting the mac and cheese in the oven, I take the seat next to Antonio and snuggle in with my caramel filled chocolates and heated blanket as Alessandro starts the first movie of the night. Since they pulled me and the countless other women from that building, I've spent a lot of time with the two of them. So much so that they've become like family to me in the span of only a few days. But I think they can tell that I'm still a little wary of their friendship, since Gio was starting to feel like a friend too before he did what he did.

This thing between the three of us feels different though. More family than friend. I can see us getting a lot closer in the coming months, especially if Braxton and I decide to see this relationship through.

TWELVE

Klara

MY **BREATH HITCHES** when Braxton emerges from the bathroom of our resort room. Jeans slung low on his hips, drops of water still cascading down his chiseled abs from his shower. This is the first time I'm seeing him in something other than a clean, crisp suit and I like. So much so that I may be drooling... just a bit.

I still can't believe this man is mine. After two years of playing his own game of catch and release he's finally mine.

"Mia Bella, keep looking at me like that and we'll never leave this room."

Grinning, I peel the blankets away slowly revealing my naked body. "Would that be so bad?" I lean back against the headboard, a hand trailing down my middle to the apex of my thighs. "We're here for two weeks, we could go exploring tomorrow... or the next day, or the day after that..."

Braxton's eyes heat, a growl reverberating through his chest when my fingers find my clit and my back arches. My eyes close on a moan as I thrust a finger into my wet heat. Strong hands grip my knees, forcing my legs apart and then Braxton's mouth is on me. His tongue licking up my slit when my hand falls away to tangle in his hair.

After all the shit we've been through over the last two years, Braxton whisked me away to Playa Del Carmen, Mexico, where we could do jack shit except for lie on the beach soaking up the sun, drinking tropical drinks all day long. Everything was included in our stay so there was no need to leave the resort if we didn't want to. And I didn't want to. I planned to get very acquainted with Braxton's body over the next two weeks while working on my tan in between. He had a couple tattoos that I was looking forward to tracing with my tongue, and I'm not just talking about the one on his ass.

"Ah, fuck!" I groan, my fingers tightening around his hair as I grind down on his mouth.

"That's it, Klara. Come on my tongue."

Something inside me coils tight and then snaps sending shudders up my body. I let go of his head and try to buck away from his mouth when his tongue continues its assault on my sensitive clit.

"So fucking beautiful," he murmurs, kissing up my body.

My legs automatically wrap around his waist when his body covers mine and he slides inside, filling me to the hilt. Braxton kisses my forehead, each of my closed eyes, my nose, the corners of my mouth, my lips parting in invitation.

"I love you, Mia Bella."

My body stills, his words taking me by surprise. I knew Braxton loved me. Everything about his actions told me he's loved me for a long time, despite his attempts to trample it down. But this is only the second time I'm hearing him say the words. Braxton runs his nose up the curve of my neck, breathing me in when my arms wrap securely around his shoulders holding him to me.

"I love you, Brax." The words leave me on a moan as Braxton takes us both over the edge.

***

"You have to try this." I push the paper plate into his hands, holding up a fork to his lips with the chocolatey goodness.

"What is it?" Braxton eyes the fork skeptically over the frame of his mirrored aviator sunglasses.

My jaw drops, eyes rounding in shock. "Have you not had a crepe before?"

"Can't say that I have. What is it?" Placing a hand on my lower back Braxton steers us toward the main building of the resort, and one of the many VIP only bars while I try to walk and eat without getting any chocolate on my white tank top.

I moan when the taste of milk chocolate and hazelnut hit my tongue, Braxton stops suddenly, turning on me and pulling me against him. It happens so fast that I barely have enough time to move the plate out of the way, saving the chocolate. Braxton's hands curl around my neck, forcing my face up to his, then his lips are on mine demanding entry.

"The next time you moan like that, Klara, will be around my cock. Understand?"

I nod, my tongue running along the bottom of my kiss swollen lips. For a split second I wonder why the fuck we're not holed up in our room exploring each other's bodies. I know Braxton wants to explore the city, but I want to explore him. All his hard edges, dips, and ridges. I want to run my tongue along the tattoo snaking up his arm from wrist to shoulder. I want to dig my nails into the hard muscle of his back as he thrusts into me. We have two missed years to make up for.

My lips curl in a mischievous grin when my eyes dart from his lips to the chocolate spilling out of the crepe. Braxton's dark eyes narrow when I swipe a finger through the warm chocolate and slowly... deliberately swirl my tongue around it before sucking it into my mouth. I make sure to moan, low and long, so only he can hear it.

Braxton swallows hard, his Adam's apple bobbing with the strained motion, seconds before his hand curls around my wrist and we're moving fast through the lobby and out to the pathway that leads up to our room.

We spend the first week lost in each other, memorizing every kiss, every nip, every touch, every breath, all the I love you's. And the next week exploring the city and all the little shops on the main road outside the resort.

I'm a mixture of disappointed and relieved when our two weeks comes to an end and we have to leave our bubble. Disappointed because I wish we could exit in the world we were in for the last two weeks, where it was just us. Braxton wasn't the Don of the mafia, and I wasn't an unemployed university grad student. For the last two weeks, Braxton was just mine and I was just his. I'm also slightly relieved because I miss our friends back home and the life we started building together.

But then as soon as we take our seats on the private jet, the screen of Braxton's phone lights up and every muscle in my body pulls tight. I really don't want to leave the bubble the resort provided because the name on the screen is the last name I ever want to hear or see for the rest of my life.

Alessandro: Located Dante.

Dante.

THIRTEEN

BRAXTON

"**H**ELLO, COUSIN," **DANTE** says as I step out of the shadows, the lone streetlight and the moon our only source of light. It shouldn't have surprised me that he knew I would come for him, and that he would hire protection.

"Was beginning to think I would have to chase you down again. I would say to put you down like a dog, but they deserve more respect, don't you think?" I cock my head to the side, taking him in in the dim lighting. Wondering why the fuck he never ran like he always would.

His face is bathed in shadows but his clothes are dirty, torn and frayed at the ends. He looks like he's fought his way through the depths of hell and back. But that means nothing to me because wherever he's been will be a cakewalk compared to what I have planned for him.

"Where's the girl?" I sense more than see his eyes darting around us, looking for any sign of life other than ours. He won't find any.

"She's none of your concern," I respond, slowly pulling my prized blade from its confines in the inside pocket of my jacket. The edge catching the light from the streetlamp. Dante goes stiff next to me.

"Did you really think it would be that easy? That I would just hand myself over to the great Braxton De Luca?"

I let out a throaty chuckle, knowing that by my now my men have taken out any threat Dante thought to place around us, and that whatever happens here tonight, whatever the surrounding businesses think they would have heard, the cops will never be called. There will be no investigation, no newspaper article. The city will go on like it always has.

"Did you really think I wouldn't find and eliminate any threat you had planted?"

My lips slowly tip up in a smirk as I look over at him. He's closer now, out of the shadows. I don't think he's even noticed the small move, but now I can see his face perfectly. The fear in his eyes, the sweat coating his brow.

"Tell me, did the bitch tell you how much she liked me fucking her? How much she begged for my dick? Said it was the best she's ever had."

Dante swallows hard at the snarl that rips through me. His lips snapping shut as he takes a step back and bumps into the chest of Alessandro. His eyes widen in shock, and I know I have him exactly where I want him. Alessandro shoves him forward until Dante is standing under the streetlight, his eyes darting between the men standing in the shadows around us, dressed in black. Each one acting like his own grim reaper.

"You really need four men to help take me out?" Dánte heaves, his chest rapidly rising and falling with every heavy breath.

"I don't need any help in taking you out, cousin. They're here to make sure you don't run." I make a show of undoing the buttons of my suit jacket and taking it off before tossing it at the man to my right before rolling up the sleeves of my dark dress shirt. Enjoying the unease emanating from him.

Dante laughs nervously, backing up into Stefan's crossed arms before he's shoved toward me. I take advantage of the split-second Dante looks behind him at the massive motherfucker that shoved him. My fist connects with the side of his face as he looks back over at me. It was a sucker punch but I don't care. Not when Dante goes down hard from the momentum, and not when he curses as the hand he presses to his nose comes away bloody.

I grip his greasy hair between my fingers and drag him up an inch before my fist connects with the side of his face again. I don't relent on my hold on hair as I deliver blow after blow. I only stop when a throat clearing sounds behind me, reminding me that I planned on dragging this out. I planned on making him suffer, planned on making him pay for each and every one of the girls we found, and for Klara. For the nightmares she tries to hide from me. She thinks I don't hear them because I've become so fucking good at controlling my breathing and pretending I'm asleep. But I hear every single one of her cries and screams. I have bruises and scratch marks on my chest from where she's held me so fucking tight in her sleep I thought she would for sure draw blood. It only got worse when she caught a glimpse of Alessandro's text about Dante. If putting my cousin down was going to help her sleep better at night then her wish was my fucking command.

I straighten up to my full height, wiping away some of the sweat from my forehead at the same time I nod at Stefan and Alessandro. The two big men grab hold of each of Dante's arms and lift him up enough for me to slice my blade through his tattered shirt until it falls away from him. His pants are next, and then they're releasing him. My fist clenches with the need to hit him again but if I start, I won't stop, and I need him to be conscious for this next part.

Stefan and Alessandro kick out each of his knees so he's forced to kneel in front of me, his head bobbing to the side from the damage my fists delivered. I move to stand beside him, gripping the hair at his nape in one of my hands and yanking on it, exposing his throat.

"This," I hiss close to his ear, "is for Ashley." I continue as I carve the little girl's name into his chest.

Antonio got me a list of names of every single one of the girls Dante had held in that run-down building. And as I finish carving one name into his skin, I move further down and start on another. Making sure he hears every single name. "This is for Jessika... This is for Robyn..." On and on it goes, until I've moved in front of him and every single inch of his skin is sporting a new name. Blood dripping from the deep wounds.

None of this will ever come close to giving those girls back their innocence, but I can at least have a hand in bringing their captor to justice. My justice. The law would have let him off too easy. A slap on the wrist and away he goes. Those girls deserved more than that. They deserved to know that the man responsible for their worst nightmare was never coming back, that he will never be able to touch them again for as long as they lived. That they were safe.

"And this…" I pause, running the tip of the blade over the sensitive flesh. "This is for Klara." The metal slices through as the last word leaves my tongue and Dante howls in pain. His blood is no longer dripping, but has now pooled around him, the appendage sitting in the puddle between his legs, and then he passes out. A collective groan sounds around the circle as each man unconsciously covers their junk with a hand.

"Was that necessary? Cutting off his dick?" Antonio asks from behind me.

"It was all necessary," I respond, cleaning the blade of the blood and snapping off the black gloves.

"What now?" Alessandro asks as we all watch Dante groan while he comes in and out of consciousness.

"Want us to take him up to the farm?" Stefan questions.

"No. I think tonight calls for a bonfire. Make it big, but clean this mess up first," I instruct, then turn on my heel and get into the blacked-out SUV and make my way home to my girl.

FOURTEEN

BRAXTON

"WHAT DOES THIS mean?" Klara asks, staring down at the ring I placed in front of her plate this morning at breakfast

"It means you get to have everything you've ever dreamt of having. The husband, the house, and maybe one day the kids."

I see the wariness forming behind her eyes when she starts to protest but I shut that shit down fast when I sweep her hair off her shoulders with my fingers, palming the side of her face. "And I get to be the lucky bastard to give it to you."

Her mouth opens and closes with unformed words and I grin. I think this is the first time Klara has had trouble coming up with a comeback, but while this feels... words cannot describe how it feels to be able to hold my heart in my arms again, she still needs to know the dangers she faces if she accepts my proposal. The daily threat to her safety will not just always be there, but it'll continue to grow.

"But Klara, life with me will never be easy. You should know that before you agree to anything. If you think I was a possessive bastard before, then you're sure to hate me once I put that ring on your finger. I'm not your knight in shining armor, Mia Bella. I'm not someone to base your dreams on." I pause, looking away momentarily.

"I know I'll be safe as long as you're with me." She places her small hands on my hips, trying to get my attention when I refuse to give her my eyes. "Braxton," she starts, her hands curling into the fabric of my shirt. "I'd stand in the shadows of your heart and tell you I'm not afraid of your dark." She grins up at me. "I read that somewhere, and since meeting you it's always just been stuck in the back of my mind. I know what I'm signing up for. I know you'll never be an easy man to love. I know this life comes with more cons than pros. I know that violence will always be a way of life. But I also know that at the end of the day, I get to curl up next to you, get to lay my head on your chest and feel your heart beat. I get to feel your arms wrap around me. Arms that I know I'll always be safe in. At the end of the day, Braxton, I get you. And that…" She reaches up on her tiptoes, her lips inches from mine. "And that is worth everything."

I press my lips against hers, savoring the feel of her pressed against me.

"And so the beauty fell in love with the beast," she grins against my lips before my tongue sweeps into her mouth, claiming what's mine.

The End

EPILOGUE

Jessika

Two years later

"**DEEP BREATHS, JESS**. In. Out. In. Out. He's just a man," I tell myself. "Just a normal person. Nothing to be afraid of."

I groan, resting my forehead against the painted wood of the apartment door I'm currently standing in front of like a stalker.

Why I decided to try and find him I have no idea. Morbid curiosity maybe? Fuck if I know. I did owe him a thank you for rescuing me from that hell though, but that doesn't explain how I tracked down his name... and his number... and his address two years after the fact.

Well... it actually did. Klara and I talked a lot while we were held at the hospital. We bonded over the darkest time in both our lives and have been in contact ever since. I may or may not have let slip while we were leaving the hospital that I wanted to thank the man who had saved me, and she hadn't hesitated to give me his name and a number I could reach him at. I had the feeling, though, that she wasn't supposed to give me that information but did anyway. She did not, however, give me his address. No, that I tracked down all by myself.

Yup, that's me. Jessika Tomlinson, stalker extraordinaire. To be fair, you can find anyone's address with a name and phone number. So, what did she expect? Probably not that I would show up on his doorstep, that was for damn sure.

I'm such an idiot. He's totally going to call the cops on me.

Just as I'm about to lift my forehead and turn around having successfully talked myself out of this stupid plan, the door swings open causing me to lose my footing and stumble forward into a very hard, very tall body. He grunts, catching me around the waist and standing me up, his hands never leaving my body until he's sure I'm steady on my feet.

"Sorry. I'm sorry. I was just-"

"Leaning against my door," he finishes for me.

"No," I cross my arms over my chest in a defiant manner. "well, maybe," I correct when one dark eyebrow raises in a try-again move.

Now that I'm standing in front of him I take a minute to take him in. He's tall. I mean massive, almost giant like. I'm five-six and he easily towers over me by another foot. His dark hair is shaved down to his head, his grey eyes are striking against his tanned skin, and holy poop talk about vein porn. The veins on his arms are fan-yourself-drool-worthy. His chest is broad, his stomach hard. I can see the ridges of his sculptured abs through the cotton of his muscle shirt when he crosses his arms.

"You about done looking your fill?"

216

Sweet Jesus, that voice. It's deep, seductive, and coupled with his physique will probably be my undoing.

"Nope," I pop the 'p' continuing my eye fuck of the specimen in front of me. You'd think after what I went through in that make shift room of that cold, dark building that eye fucking a man, let alone thinking about all the things I'd like to do to him would be the last thing on my mind. But over the last two years after realization sunk in that I wasn't living in that nightmare anymore I've had a tough time thinking of anything other than the man who saved me from hell.

Strong hands grip my wrist, yanking me into the strong body my eyes were just perusing. "Did you come here to dance with the devil, Jessika?"

My breath hitches as I stare up into colorless eyes. "How did you know my name?"

"After two years, I know more than just your name sweetheart."

"You've been stalking me?"

His other hand moves down to the dip at my lower back applying just enough pressure to bring me closer into his body. "Like you've been stalking me?"

"I came to say thank you."

He smirks, dipping his head and brushing his lips along my jaw turning my knees to jello, and if he wasn't holding me up, I'm certain I would've melted into a pool of need at his feet. "Haven't thanked me yet but if eye fucking me from across the room is your way of saying thank you, I'm going to need a lot more than that." His tongue licks up my jaw, his teeth nipping at my ear lobe causing me to shiver.

I swallow hard, my panties already growing damp. "Thank you."

"For what?" His breath is warm against my skin.

His lips hover just above mine and I have to fight back a moan. "For saving me."

Abruptly he pulls away, taking those lips and the heat of his body with him as he takes several steps backward. I have to stop myself when I realize I'm seconds away from pouting and demanding he continue what he started. I watch him gather his wallet, keys, and holster a handgun before throwing on a leather jacket.

"Got somewhere to be, babe."

I follow him out thinking we can continue a conversation as we both head downstairs but as soon as he locks the apartment door behind us, he turns in the opposite direction and stalks off toward the stairs so fast that it leaves my head spinning. By the time I've recovered enough to follow him, he's gone.

***

(Alessandro)

I needed to get out of there and fast because as soon as I saw her, got my hands on her I wanted to claim her. Fuck, I wasn't ready for her to find me. I wasn't prepared for the tornado that is Jessika Tomlinson, but ready or not she was here. And now that I've had my hands on her again I don't plan on letting go this time.

Prepare yourself, Jess. You're about to tango with the devil's second-in-command.

PLAYLIST

https://open.spotify.com/.../.../playlist/4w5FrH
hNgs5LlI4pYAa7Vj

Let Me Go – Hailee Steinfeld
Should've Been Us – Tori Kelly
The Devil's Bleeding Crown – Volbeat
Moth Into Flame – Metallica
Smooth Criminal – Michael Jackson
Hello – Evanescence
FMLYHM – Seether
Les Memoires Blessees – Dark Sanctuary
Ashes To Ashes – Nox Arcana
Path of Shadows – Nox Arcana
King of Fools – Nox Arcana
Dark Desire – Nox Arcana
No Stopping You – Brett Eldredge
Here Without You – 3 Doors Down
If You Only Knew – Shinedown
How You Like Me Now- The Heavy
Beautiful Hell – Adna
Starving – Hailee Steinfeld
Bad Things – Machine Gun Kelly ft. Camila Cabello
Blue Moon – Damian Syslo
Workin' On Whiskey – Jessica Mitchell
Drink You Away – Trent Harmon
I Can't Fell In Love Without You – Zara Larsson

Body On Me- Rita Ora
Sober – Lorde
Turning Page – Sleeping At Last
Can't Keep Waiting – Autumn Hill
Let Me Go – 3 Doors Down
Good To You – Marianas Trench
Not Meant To Be – Theory of a Deadman
Read Me My Rights – Brantley Gilbert
Creepin' – CID
Instruction – Jax Jones

MORE

Behind These Eyes Series (Can be read as standalones)
Skin Deep (January 2017)
Piece of Me (no longer available)
Always You (September 2017)

A Famiglia series (Can be read as standalones)
Dark Desire (January 2018)
Dark Redemption
Dark Betrayal
Dark Illusion
Deadly Addiction

ABOUT

You can take the girl out of the ocean but you cannot take the ocean out of the girl. A.J believes that describes her to a T. She practically grew up on a beach in Cape Town, South Africa until her family immigrated to Canada. However, the ocean still has a way of relaxing her. If she can't get to the water, then a long drive with the music blaring will work just fine.

She wears her heart on her sleeve and is a self-proclaimed hopeless romantic who believes that everyone deserves their happily ever after. A.J. lives in BC, Canada with her husband. When she's not writing, she's reading. She loves the NFL and drinks way too much coffee.

If you enjoyed reading Dark Desire, please leave a review on your favorite book retailer and/or Goodreads.

Connect with A.J.

FACEBOOK: facebook.com/adanielsauthor
FACEBOOK READER GROUP: A.J.'S NAUGHTY ANGELS
INSTAGRAM: instagram.com/a.j_daniels_author
TWITTER: twitter.com/AJDanielsAuthor
WEBSITE: http://ajdanielsauthor.weebly.com/

Made in the USA
Monee, IL
12 June 2020

33459853R00142